I0817698

ALSO BY DANIEL POPPICK

Fear of Description

The Police

THE COPYWRITER

A Novel

DANIEL POPPICK

SCRIBNER

New York Amsterdam/Antwerp London
Toronto Sydney/Melbourne New Delhi

Scribner
An Imprint of Simon & Schuster, LLC
1230 Avenue of the Americas
New York, NY 10020

This book is a work of fiction. As is true in many books of fiction, this book was inspired by real events. Nevertheless, all of the actions in the book, as well as all of the characters and dialogue are products solely of the author's imagination.

First Scribner hardcover edition February 2026

Interior design by Jaime Putorti

Manufactured in the United States of America

1 3 5 7 9 10 8 6 4 2

Library of Congress Cataloging-in-Publication Data is available.

ISBN 978-1-6680-9000-8
ISBN 978-1-6680-8999-6 (ebook)

For Andy and Laura

AUTHOR'S NOTE

I believe in the reality of absent things. If something isn't here, it must be somewhere else.

Fate: how the absent thing remains lost.

Serendipity: how the absent thing returns.

Fiction: how we make it up.

Poetry: how we wait for it.

Everyone wants to be a poet to ghost on a code: be it money, love, deadly empire, a politics of grace or winking futurity, poetry thrills because it spirits you away from what you thought you were, into the heart of the dominant x.

It's not important that we "have" no fucks left to give: we are ourselves the fuck-void. And inside this fuck-void's event horizon is a zone where all things trickle through—light, sound, matter, and time itself. A collapsed star.

Observations, longings, parables, aphorisms, dreams, stories, news, jokes, fragments of speech overheard or invented, questions, lists, lyrics, doggerel, dictates, emails, bullshit, bellwethers, lies. Notes.

What follows is a work of fiction. But if it makes nothing happen, call it poetry.

So what I believed to be nothing was simply my entire life.

—MARCEL PROUST, *THE FUGITIVE*

(for time, like money, is measured by our needs)

—GEORGE ELIOT, *MIDDLEMARCH*

SUMMER NOTEBOOK, 2017

JUNE

The wind erases a line in the sand.

Parable of the New CEO

The company I work for recently got a new CEO. He is twenty-four years old and has never managed a company before, but he is charismatic; when he looks at me during our private two-hour coffee break, a conversation he is having with every single employee to "get to know us better," I feel his time matters.

"Everything we do needs to have heart," he says near the end of this meeting. "When someone writes a negative review of their lavender-scented yoga mat, we need to ask ourselves how we could have strengthened our connection with that person. When we pack up and ship our customers the 'Yas Queen' throw pillows, we need to affirm them the way they affirm themselves. When we write a description of the eggplant emoji drone, we need to be anticipating how that product makes our customers feel—would highlighting the Bluetooth speaker installed in the tip connect someone more deeply to their joy in the moment they read about it on our site? I don't know, D__, you're the writer—*you* tell *me*. From here on out everything we do is going to have heart."

Transfixed, I agree—and, oddly, not just because my job depends on it.

"Tell me, D__," he says, sipping cold brew from a straw. "What kind of poetry do you write?" And just like that, the spell is broken. It is only now that I start to dislike him.

At this point I should really have an answer to this question, but I do not. I give him my stock answer: "Most of it doesn't rhyme." But then I remember that, come to think of it, there *is* a lot of internal rhyme in my recent work, and add, idiotically, "But recently a lot of it does."

He continues as if I haven't spoken—as if what I just said was uttered outside of time. "I'm going to ask that tomorrow everyone bring in a product that means something to them. Really *means* something to you"—narrowing his eyes as if to switch the italics on in his voice—"you know?"

I don't. "Yes, of course."

"Good. Bring it in tomorrow and we'll talk about it."

When I get back to my desk, I Google:

> what is a product

I do not pride myself on being a savvy professional operator, but after a decade of attending poetry readings, I have learned a thing or two about power-hungry nihilists who for one reason or another need to believe themselves to be gentle. It is clear that someone is going to be fired as a result of this meeting, which is in fact a test, and I resolve that it will not be me.

Directly after work I walk across Tribeca to a used bookstore and buy the rattiest, ugliest available copy of Lewis Hyde's *The Gift*, an anthropological study of "gift economies." The subtitle of this older edition, omitted from more recent ones, is "Imagination and the Erotic Life of Property." Perfect.

In the meeting the next day, my colleagues present earrings, an appealingly faded denim jacket, picture frames, a hair clip—the CEO is especially impressed by the hair clip—a notebook, and a synth keyboard. My turn comes around. I present the volume of *The Gift* as my personal copy, one I've owned for many years, and explain that I value this book over other property because it has taught me to see hitherto invisible webs of relationality when I shop on the internet, and that the material sustaining these relations—in human commerce, but also among plants and fungi, even rocks—is time itself, the most precious commodity imaginable. I note that I also love the vintage font on the cover.

My colleagues look confused, but the CEO does not. "That is not a product," he says. "It might be a prized possession. It might be a book." He lets a dramatic silence fill the conference room. I pray that the meeting will end with that observation, but he is just getting ready to drive his point home. "And yet it is not a product."

Nearly anyone who attempts to publish their writing learns, often in humiliating and painful fashion, that to most of the world a book is a product designed to give its reader a narrow set of experiences. This is a brutally restricted way of imagining literature, and much else—but even within this potentially soul-killing purview, an entire ecosystem has survived, tenaciously, for centuries. Yet to our CEO an unfashionable, worn-out volume advancing even the mildest critique of capitalism could not be a product, because he cannot imagine the person who would use this particular book as a hair clip. That is my advantage.

After the meeting ends, I follow him into his office. "Can I talk to you?" I say.

"Yes, of course, D__." He smiles tightly.

"I was thinking about what you were saying about everything we do needing to have heart. I'd like for you to have this." I slide the book across his desk. "My only request is that after you're finished reading it you pass it on, which I think is in keeping with the spirit of the book and what you're trying to bring to this company. It feels relevant to what we've been talking about. I think you'll really love it."

He regards me anew.

This is not a story about fate. It is a story about serendipity.

"Thank you so much," he says. "I will. Noted."

I meet his gaze as he waits for me, like a dune waits for wind, to speak.

I'm not a religious person, but sometimes I find myself in a situation that seems concocted elsewhere—in a parallel dimension, created by an intelligence with narrative omniscience. John Ashbery wrote, "Everything has a schedule, if you can find out what it is." In these seemingly concocted moments, it feels as if some presence is trying to teach me a schedule, should I wish to learn. And I do wish to learn, but I never find out what it is—in fact I am rarely aware of learning anything, in any situation, ever. But I do know a good story when it falls into my lap.

But it's not just stories. I'll overhear someone saying something that seems to suggest an entire reality splintering off from reality as I know it—like the other day when I was walking by the steps of the courthouse in downtown Brooklyn on the way to the subway, a red-faced man in a crisply pressed suit muttered into his phone, "There were all sorts of civil rights I didn't expect the extent of."

And sometimes it's not overheard language, but language that seems transmitted to me via radio signal. When I remember a dream, it will often simply be a disembodied phrase in a distinct, unidentifiable voice, like "What audible skin you have!" as if spoken by a midwestern banker. And it's not just dreams. Sometimes it's not language-based at all but an idea, like the idea that the alphabet could physically cast shade on a sunny day; or a sound, a piece of music, a particular toll of a bell.

I feel that if I follow the logic of these moments a bit farther, I will discover the answer to a great riddle, but if I follow them too far I will never find my way back to my own life.

Our company is deeply "in the red," a phrase I've always loved. Another way of saying it might be that our company "isn't making enough money," is perhaps even "hemorrhaging money," or "isn't creating objects imbued with value, or 'heart,' sufficient to motivate customers to exchange their hard-earned fungible assets for ownership, because the kitsch status pieces that we sell are last season's kitsch status pieces, otherwise known as garbage; and because these customers' fungible assets are vital to the company's continued survival, the company, our company, is teetering on the edge of ruin."

A breeze blows through the CEO's open window, scattering a few loose sheets of paper across the office. The CEO, rattled and caught off-balance as if for the first time in his life, smiles at me again and frantically tries to gather them. I take this opportunity to leave.

I reheat last night's leftovers in the microwave and cheerfully return to my desk to eat. I sink my teeth into what can only be described as the Versailles of meat loaf.

Layoffs have been widely expected all month. But the next day the new CEO doesn't show up. Or the next. Or the next. He disappears from the office like a puddle in extractive sun. The word we are all awaiting never comes.

I drape myself, in realist fashion, with my laptop and a small cup of Keurig-brewed coffee, across the gray chaise longue by the ferns, trying to imagine what people who are in the market for a coat hook shaped like a panda want to believe about themselves.

"I liked that denim jacket you brought in for the meeting," I say to my colleague Fatima the next week in the office kitchen.

"Aw, thanks," she says. She returns to her desk, shoes clapping across the linoleum floor.

After that, it is as if the ritual we had all taken part in had never occurred at all. That's why I need to write things down.

JULY

I am already awake when the alarm goes off—our two cats stirred me at four a.m., batting at the blinds and wailing at nothing. I wonder how being chronically sleep-deprived affects my personality, but on a day-to-day level I'm used to it. Lucy turns to me half-asleep and says, "I dreamed James Gandolfini was masturbating in the sky."

I brush the hair from her face. "Are you anxious about something?"

She sighs. "Just work."

I reach for my notebook on the nightstand, scribble "I dreamed T. Soprano masturbating sky."

Lucy gives me a suspicious look. "Are you writing my dream in your diary?"

"It's not a diary."

"Are you writing my Gandolfini dream in your dream journal?"

"It's not a journal, it's a notebook. And if you're not going to use it, yeah, I might. Can I?"

She shakes her head. "You should try recording your own dreams, but sure."

"If I dreamed James Gandolfini was masturbating in the sky, I would write it down. You've been given a gift and you're not even going to use it in a poem?"

"It's true, I'm not going to use that in a poem."

A notebook is a performance for one person: the person writing it. But in becoming my own audience, I always become someone else. Even when I describe reality in minute detail, there is always a whiff of bullshit on the breeze. Private writing for an imagined public. A waste of time.

Parable of Story

Almost everyone I know outside of work is a poet. Lucy and I have lived together for six years. We bonded over poetry in grad school when I was getting an MFA and she was pursuing a PhD, writing a dissertation on the use of live animals in post-Elizabethan theater—mostly sheep, but occasionally dogs and pigs—which she later abandoned for a job at a magazine. Will, who not long ago finished his own PhD with a dissertation on the poetics of bureaucracy and ekphrasis that his advisor told him was the best she'd ever read, works as a deliveryman for an office furniture supply company, because there are no jobs in academia—likewise, a poet. And Ruth, who until recently was living on the stipend of a prestigious writing fellowship, is moving to LA this month, also to pursue a PhD—also a poet. We gather for a send-off dinner in her honor at Lucy's and my place.

"I'm done," Ruth says over a quarter of a plate of roasted cauliflower, delivering the words like a lithe boxer elegantly working a punching bag. One of our cats, the bullseye tabby, jumps on the table and in a single motion I mindlessly pick him up and throw him on the couch, where he emits a soft meep upon impact. Lucy reaches for Ruth's plate. "Oh, I meant I'm done with poetry," says Ruth. "But you can take the plate. Thank you, it was delicious."

"What do you think that—means? That you're done with poetry," Will says with edgy patience, lighting a joint. He and Ruth dated years ago, then got over it and stayed friends. He takes a deep toke and passes it to her.

"No thanks," she says, hitting the joint anyway before passing it to me. "Of course I'm not *done* with it. But I do feel that my—our—apprenticeship in it is coming to an end. I'm no longer interested in fractured syntax, or even language's materiality."

"Like your poem that revealed the message 'U BE' is contained in the word 'PUBE'?" Will says. "I do prefer your newer stuff."

"That was not mine!"

“I liked that poem,” Lucy says, returning to the table.

“It had something,” I say, “but that was Chester’s poem.”

“You were into that kind of thing for a minute,” Will says.

“I had an Aram Saroyan phase in my twenties like everyone else. God, Chester was bad. Is he still hot? I should text him when I get to LA. Anyway, I’m more interested in poetry that comes from someone’s actual life. Narrative! Why was it that we wrote off the confessionalists?” Ruth scratches the head of our other cat, the Russian blue, as he purrs.

“Because they were all boring, racist, and killed themselves?” Will says.

“I love Anne Sexton,” Lucy says.

“Lowell is disgusting,” Will says. “Except for his translation of that one Baudelaire poem where he uses the word ‘fuck.’ That was a good choice.” We all nod.

“Look, voice emerges from syntax,” Ruth says. “Syntax from character, character from a particular time and place. A story strings itself together with that combination of elements.” Out of nowhere, her eyes roll back as if she is about to be taken by the rapture. “Guys! When I’m talking to you it feels exactly like writing—like I’m just talking to my computer.”

“I’m stealing that,” I say.

"You're welcome."

"Most of my poems these days are just lists," I say, to annoy her. "Can a list be a story?"

"A list is an inventory, and behind every inventory—"

"When Rihanna sings 'work, work, work, work, work, work,'" Lucy interrupts, "that's a pretty amazing story."

"It is, especially when Drake then goes, 'you need to get done, done, done.'" Ruth laughs.

I'm sad Ruth is leaving. The end of an era. The four of us have made a little family for ourselves. We've seen each other through some kind of crisis. But of what? Faith?

In what?

The night, like a cat, suffers from resting void face.

What are you here for, cat, if not for us to project *Love Streams* onto? And not in a poetic sense: I mean I'd like to project the final film by John Cassavetes onto your enormous torso while you swat at the light. Then finally you might know what some people go through.

Questions to Which the Answer Is "Night"

With what instrument does one best see the instrument?
What time is the right time?
Which watchman?

The only thing bigger than the idea of hell is its shape. Its flames catch your face in its outer ring, and your face becomes hell's satellite. Otherwise your face is just your face.

Some say there's no such thing as the muse. I'm inclined to believe that the muse does exist, though we may not like it when we meet it. For example, Will's new translation of the opening of *The Iliad*:

Okay Google, what's rage?

I sometimes wonder what made us poets in the first place. Did we accidentally sell our souls to the devil when we were children, without realizing it?

I vividly remember a children's film from the late eighties, about a goose befriending a donkey, entitled *Dido & Anus.* Though this film doesn't actually exist, it has made an impression on me.

What unites these animals? (a) An inborn facility with human speech. (b) An ambivalent relationship with all labor associated with "carrying a load." (c) Nostalgia for a farm in a neighboring valley where both once rolled among bluebells long ago—a nostalgia that only the most sensitive child correctly interprets, happily stuffing his face with Oreos on a Saturday night in front of a TV while a babysitter nods off on the couch, as a coy invitation from Satan himself to record the world verbally, as an aid to memory.

"Can I put you down as a reference on my LA rental applications?" Ruth asks. "I'd list you as my friend—and colleague—because it's true! They just need your name and number." I'm startled to realize that she's right. Poetry has rendered us colleagues.

The colleague is the sunlight of the bureaucratic form; the friend is the rain; their names and numbers the seeds that put up pale shoots in the flat, bleached soil.

Being there to see it happen: your friends, events, and atoms.

Walking into the office, I hear a dial tone in my limbs. The drone of desire, gilded with anticipation.

Fatima looks up and stops typing, seemingly hypnotized by the pink foam cube radiating in a patch of sunlight by the ferns and water cooler.

"What's up?" I ask after a moment.

"I was just thinking about this cool gray couch I want for my apartment," she says, blinking and continuing to type, "and what it would be like if I ended up living on the street."

An autocorrect for flowers: obviously useless. But what about an autocorrect for the money one used to buy those flowers? For the time before the first petal drops?

Am I "in my youth" or its theater of cruelty?

"I hit my peak as a writer in third grade," Ruth says as I am driving her to the airport. "Those poems were good. They were about real things. Ferrets. Immigration. Poachers in Wyoming. The Industrial Revolution, the Bread and Roses Strike of 1912, the state of Texas. You've seen the anthology my mom put together."

"You're anxious because you think getting a PhD will cut you off from your own poetry," I diagnose in monotone autopilot, squinting at the traffic, "but it can only feed—motherfucker!" A car cuts me off as I try to change lanes.

"Wow," she says, biting a hangnail. "You might only be half-wrong." She surveys her hand. "But it's not really academia that I'm worried will cut me off from poetry."

We ride on in silence for a while. As I pull up to the curb at JFK, I say, "What *could* cut you off from poetry?"

She suddenly looks like she's about to cry, but she just shrugs and smiles. "Thanks for the ride. Take care of Will and Lucy."

She grabs her suitcases and drags them into the airport.

Parable of He

He loved the alphabet. But what he loved more was the alphabet's shade.

He arranged his calendar, his poems, and his notes like a vase of corrected flowers.

AUGUST

When I was growing up and preparing for my bar mitzvah, I remember asking the rabbi at our temple if he believed in God. He laughed and said, "What do you think?"

None of the adults around me seemed to give a flying fuck about God, Jewish or otherwise, but there was a mysterious motivation behind their thinking that I wanted to understand. Why did they tell us we could be anything we wanted to be when we grew up when they had jobs they clearly hated? Why would one of them insist on paying for dinner as soon as another produced a credit card at a restaurant? Why did they think I should want to read *The Lord of the Rings*, which was boring and anti-Semitic, and that I shouldn't want to watch *The Simpsons*, which was funny and taught me about society? Why did they say everyone deserved to be treated equally, but that this was "complicated" when it came to people without money and Palestinians?

Every Saturday we toasted our personal-sized loaves of bread and spread cream cheese around their holes. In every sense the hole was what we worshipped. My question to the rabbi was reasonable. So was his reply.

A few times a year I meet my parents in Manhattan for dinner, a trip to a museum, or a tasteful Off-Broadway show—we don't do musicals. Tonight, near the end of the play to which my mom secured us tickets months in advance, I notice them asleep next to me, their heads turned to the part of the stage where the actors are now screaming at one another. As the screaming actors walk across the stage and into the wings as the curtain goes down, my parents' sleeping heads turn with them. The lights go up. The audience claps. My parents open their eyes.

"Culture," my dad says, blinking. I wait for him to finish. He pats my knee and gives it a squeeze.

"That was too experimental," my mom says. "The plot didn't make sense at all."

Scrolling through the news on my laptop at the office, I read that a woman has been killed in the street by a white nationalist in Virginia—she'd been there protesting a mass gathering of torch-bearing Klansmen and neo-Nazis heartened by the rise of our fascist president, who goes on to lament that an event attended by "many fine people on both sides" was spoiled by this unfortunate incident.

A shiver slides through me—a feeling not quite rage, but just parallel to rage. Then, from a different part of my screen, I receive an email notification requesting a product description for an LED light box emblazoned with the phrase NAMASTE IN BED.

Office ekphrasis: the typo in the product description for the designer throw pillow that boasts of delivering "an object lesion in luxury" might be beautiful. But it is not art.

Office ekphrasis: the overt language of the fern by the sofa. Its typos are all over the floor.

Office ekphrasis: a sculpture of a chair that is also just a chair. A chair that is art's typo.

When you sit in it, you are described.

The CEO returns to the office once or twice a week, but when he's there we barely see him. When we do, he nods and says hello in a small, humiliated voice; not so much a voice as an indentation in the air around his mouth, a pile of rusted wheels in a junkyard, a few ghostly dandelions cutting through.

I am tasked with writing a product description for a designer sandcastle-building kit for adults, complete with several tastefully colored buckets and ergonomically correct plastic digging implements. The image shows a beach party, models about my age with rippling abs kneeling over manicured, cylindrical walls of sand. One of the models is winking, holding a small box labeled MOMMY JUICE, with a straw. Adults of my generation—traumatized by the disastrous economy that awaited us when we graduated college—are in a lifelong process of self-infantilization. Many of us are too afraid to have children of our own.

I think of a sequence of words so stupid I can barely bring myself to type them. But I know from experience that this feeling means I've landed on a keeper. I email my creative director:

> Feeling pail? Dig this: you need sun, and a castle to call your own . . .

Within minutes, it is on the website, where it will have more readers than my poems ever will.

Parable of Reading

"This is my son, Pail."

"Well hello there! You actually look rather sunburned. Have you been at the beach?"

"Yes, in fact he has been at the beach. But I didn't say 'pale.' I said Pail."

"Oh, I'm sorry—you mean as in a small bucket?"

"Yes, like a small bucket one might fill with crabs."

"I see now."

"I hope so. Do you have something against my son?"

"No, I apologize for not understanding before. It's not that I—no.

I wouldn't say I hate your son. I wouldn't. It's just that—hear me out on this—understanding his name is so much like reading. And if the question is about reading, and not your son, then the answer is yes, reading is something that I do loathe. Very deeply."

"Well, on that point I couldn't agree more. Perhaps you could think of his name as a little object. A useful object. 'Pail.' Like 'sail,' as in the boat—and *not* the exchange of goods or currency."

"I'm sorry, but that name is not a useful object."

MY OTHER PORSCHE IS A FORESKIN reads the bumper sticker I receive from an extremely organized, professional-looking anti-circumcision group handing them out on Broadway and Canal.

But where would I put this sticker?

Parable of the Eclipse

All summer, the nation has been abuzz about the full solar eclipse, the last time we will be in the path of totality until 2024—and by then, given the way things are going, perhaps we will be living in nuclear winter, without a clear view of the sky. So we have to make this one count.

Tribeca floods with people cutting out of their jobs. It had been difficult to find the tinted glasses earlier in the week—every store sold out—but in the end, people share. Someone hands me a pair, which I give to someone else. One by one, my colleagues file out of our building to join the masses pointing at the sky and the municipal flowers wilting in punishing August heat under a spray of crescent-shaped shadows. Our CEO is the only one who doesn't join us for the supreme astronomical event, which even our fascist president wants to see so badly that he is caught on film trying to stare directly into the sun.

Parable of Business Casual

The employee, dressed in rags, squints at a pyramid shimmering in the distance. A sphinx sits over him, blindly pawing in search of a lost phone. A faint ringing echoes from the pyramids. The sphinx turns to the employee, then looks toward the ringing.

"I don't even have anything to wear for this," the employee sighs, the sun beating down on him as the sand stretches out ahead.

No art, no melody, no time that is not bound up in some dark labor.

FALL NOTEBOOK, 2017

SEPTEMBER

All happy commutes are alike; each unhappy commute is unhappy in its own way. And in any case, all offices are a tomb for daylight and paper.

The train siphons him into his rhyme, his tomb.

We get daily emails from his account describing the company's finances in terms designed to obscure more than they reveal—a revelation of a different nature. We are clearly expected to do our jobs, but also to understand the unsaid: the end is near.

I recognize the dynamics of this moment in my professional life, which isn't to say I don't hate it. Understanding the unsaid, decoding silence, reaching beyond reason for what Keats called negative capability. It isn't poetry, but poetry has trained me for it.

Poetry: the art of turning away from labor while performing it.

So we continue working. Working and rotting as beautifully as rain rots off a thunderhead, dripping down our skulls as we try to protect our black, personal-pan LCD screen exocaskets from ruinous moisture.

News used to be delivered to one's door, printed on thin paper. Nowadays it simply penetrates the face, to be printed on our brains, where it rots.

I check my phone late on Sunday and see the news that is not the news. John Ashbery is dead at the age of ninety.

Poets are fractious. Even among my friends, when it comes to poetry itself, we argue constantly and agree about very little. But in Ashbery's poetry, our disagreement assumes the air of a playful conspiracy. Many of his lines are so infused in our shared sense of logic, so embalmed in our jokes—"her boyfriend's head was a green bag of narcissus stems," I say to Lucy whenever I forget to take out the trash—that they feel only half written by him. To say goodbye to him means saying goodbye, on some level, to each other.

I try to weep but can't. I splash some cold water on my face and go into the kitchen to make dinner. Everything has a schedule, if you can find out what it is.

When I can, I send a little freelance copywriting work to Will. It doesn't pay much, but it's easy money. The Tuesday after Ashbery's death, I receive a group of product descriptions from him.

• Space moves in four directions: up, down, and side to side. That's what makes this white imitation marble bookcase so useful. When you place objects on it—not only books, but also things—they stay still but go literally everywhere.

• Have you ever seen a lamp that didn't produce enough light, and over a long period of time it ruined your eyes? Not this lamp. This lamp produces just enough, all while mostly being made of wood.

• When you think of dish racks, you should think of post-modernity, because postmodern theory is often arid—or, in layman's terms, dry. Which is exactly what you want your dishes to be before you use them again. This dish rack looks like almost nothing from far away, across a large public square full of people going about their drab existence, particularly when the view is obscured by rain. But when you get close, in a kitchen, you'll see that it has a tray for runoff water—either from rainfall or your kitchen sink—and is made of smaller, interlocking squares. It makes you think.

• A scent like the ghostly hum of an electric vehicle waiting at a traffic light, a vehicle bearing children just released from a rehearsal of a school musical like *Into the Woods*, children whose hearts are swollen to the point of bursting with sophisticated song but are still well behaved, cirrus clouds stretching out over the dusk-blackened landscape beyond your windshield like affectionate, white-winged reptiles beckoning you home—that's the scent of this soy-based candle, featuring a cedar wick that crackles softly as it burns.

• The era of normal umbrellas is over. That's why this umbrella isn't normal: it's kind of cool. This is a cool umbrella.

I walk into an empty conference room and call Will.

"Yeah?" he answers.

"Hey man—how are you holding up?"

"Oh, fine. A little sad but hanging in."

"I know what you mean. Listen, sorry to change the subject—thank you for those product descriptions. I think we need to—it's not that they aren't right, we just need to make a few tweaks, so don't be offended if you see them up on the site and they aren't exactly as you wrote them. Is that cool?"

"Of course. I'm not precious about them."

"You get it. Thank you. If you submit your invoice today, the payment should come through next Wednesday."

"Perfect. Do you and Lucy want to come over tonight and read Ashbery aloud? Maybe 'Clepsydra'? I'd rather not be alone."

Under my breath, on the subway ride to Will's, I recite one of the only Ashbery poems I have memorized, "The Chateau Hardware," one of my favorites. As I get to the lines "It was the great 'as though,' the how the day went / The excursions of the police / As I pursued my bodily functions . . ." I notice a cop staring at me.

Cops give me the creeps, but when I meet his gaze, a rageful happiness overtakes me, and I smile at him.

He turns away.

I finish the poem: ". . . turning out the way I am, turning out to greet you."

Lucy and Will and I gather and Ruth joins us from California via FaceTime. When we're done reading Ashbery, we decide to write a poem of our own together.

Ruth starts, pulling a line out of the air, "The postcard was invited to the sea."

Lucy follows, "The river sent the postcard to the sea."

Then Will, "The river wrote on the sea as if it were a postcard."

Then me, "The river was our intern."

"There's not enough tension here, it's just turning into one of your list poems." Lucy laughs. "What happens to the intern?"

About a decade ago, I had a handful of internships, which at the time were generally understood to be the gateway to a career. None of them paid anything, and I lived with my parents during the summers I "worked." The fact that I had the privilege to afford this situation—supportive parents who ensured that I had no debt after college, summers' worth of résumé-padding nonemployment—filled me with shame. But not enough shame to motivate me to do a good job. I assumed that if my employers actually needed me, I would be paid, and so the work they gave me must be meaningless. It was certainly boring. The organizations where I interned—a couple of literary magazines, a nonprofit that ran creative writing workshops—contended that they could not sustain the financial pressure of paying interns. After the recession, when I was past the intern phase of my apprenticeship with professional life, having given up hope of finding work connected to poetry, New York passed a law forcing almost all these organizations to pay their interns. Miraculously, many of them have survived.

Walking home from the subway, I overhear a man with a tumescent, fatherly physique stretching his arm behind his head and saying to his phone, "My problem is I have a pretty tight window."

I only pray it all leads somewhere good—this sad, cyborgian alloy of cause and effect.

My blue metallic face surveys the pavement beneath my feet.

As I'm grief-chugging a Pamplemousse La Croix on the couch, Lucy sits down and kisses my neck.

I turn to her. "Oh?"

She smiles. We both know the drill.

As I am going down on her, a presence rises from my gut, ghostly and tactile, citrusy, pure atmosphere. No, I think—Lucy and I have been together long enough that the horizon of physical intimacy is nearly boundless, but burping while giving head would be the vanishing point.

I pause and tilt my torso back, so the carbonation slides back. I return to Lucy. I pause again, tilt my neck, shift my core. Lucy, who has been nonresponsive, gently pats my head.

"It's fine, love," she says. "I think the moment's over."

She pulls her underwear up and instantly flips open her laptop on the coffee table, cuing up *All About Eve*, which she only watches when she's sad.

I go into the bathroom, turn on the sink, and wait to hear the voice-over from the other room before releasing a belch, my enemy, sustained and silent, a long ribbon unfurling from my gut into the air.

Parable of Bach

A new genre of breathing is invented called "Bach"—breath in counterpoint with song. The breathing of someone who is of two or three minds.

Lucy and I go to see the *Goldberg Variations* performed live. A third of the way through, unexpectedly, by some reflex, I begin weeping in the theater.

At the gates of the underworld, tossing my songs into the maw of a three-headed dog.

To give them harmony, or to put them to sleep?

I miss a call from my dad while I'm at work. As I listen to the voicemail, cold dread creeps over me, swiftly pitching to panic: "Hi D__. When you get a chance, we need to discuss something important regarding my health—and potentially yours. Please call when you get a chance."

I walk quickly into an empty conference room, my hands going numb. My dad's father died of prostate cancer when he was slightly older than my dad is now. As the phone rings, I rapidly try to calibrate to a new reality: hospitals, bedpans, slow-moving and somber trips to his favorite museums—the most boring museums in the world. Every Saturday morning I opted to watch cartoons instead of playing catch with him flashes before me. I've been a terrible son.

"Listen," he says when he picks up. "I'm not sure how to say this because I'm fuzzy on the exact medical terminology—"

"Don't worry," I interrupt, trying and failing to be patient with him, "just give me the gist."

"Well, I just went to the dentist to get my teeth cleaned. The hygienist told me something interesting. Important, actually. Flossing—I didn't realize this—it's good for your entire body. I'm going to be blunt. I know you don't floss every day. You need to start doing that. And you need to visit the dentist regularly. One of your wisdom teeth is still knocking around in there. Remember that? It could come out infected at any moment."

All of this is true. I don't floss, I don't go to the dentist regularly, and only three of my four wisdom teeth have been removed—my small, brave acts of resistance against bourgeois norms. Relief washes over me, my hands now shaking. "You're right. Thanks for the reminder. I will."

"Good. Mom wants to talk to you."

My mom gets on the phone. Her father, my only living grandparent, isn't doing well. He turns one hundred in January, and dementia is taking its toll. We should plan to visit him before then, just in case.

"The sadder the words, the meaner," I write on social media while I'm stoned, then delete it. By "meaner," I don't mean "crueler"—I mean fatter in meaning, as a rain cloud or a paragraph fattens with information. But you can't expect people to get that.

Ignorant water. Officious little alphabet. Pink paragraph, drifting west at sunset. I lay me down as the rain starts to fall, to greet the budding worms.

Half the time I erased my comments from the feed. More rarely I sang what I had just erased into the blank Rolodex of evening. More rarely still, evening's contacts returned my call.

Half of grief is retrospective, and half is speculative; grief is so sci-fi.

Each word a shovelful of dirt tossed on a coffin.

His syllables clack together like small stones.

After John Ashbery

Animate, flesh-hectored
And so alphabetic
He exited his skin

And stepped outside
To a driving rain
Counted the voided

Mum stalks and walked
Up the sodden path to the road
Down which he started

North, stone fruit under tongue
His feet full of problems
And a song in their plan

OCTOBER

Admire the guillotine for its restraint.

Fatima and I are summoned to our creative director's office for a mysterious meeting. We approach the glass partition of her north-facing office wall. She is on the phone.

"I don't like this," Fatima says. The creative director waves us inside.

"Thank you," she chimes, and hangs up. Her voice drops. "It's off," she says.

"What's off?" Fatima says.

"Firing you. He told me to forget about it."

Fatima looks pale. I try to process this.

"We—were going to be fired today?" I say.

"Look, off the record, yes. But I just had the weirdest conversation with him. He was talking about something like—gift economies? And wanting everyone to have severance over the holidays? But it's going to happen eventually. Soon. God, I'm sorry, this is so unprofessional."

"Extremely unprofessional," Fatima says, "but ethical."

"Thanks," says the creative director. "I'm trying to be a better person."

"When can we expect to be fired?" I say.

"It's not just you. It's everyone. We're all getting laid off in a couple of months. One of us might stay on for website maintenance. We'll see. Maybe it could be me. Maybe one of you."

"Thank you. That means a lot to me," Fatima says.

Saying new expletives into a mirror in the inventory closet—a new mirror designed to look secondhand.

"It's going to be fine," Lucy says when I tell her that night. "Whatever happens, we'll support one another."

"I'm going to lose my job," I say. "It's not going to be fine."

"You knew that this would happen. You've been saving for it," Lucy points out. This is true. The company was so dysfunctional from the start that for some time I've been operating under the assumption that every week would be my last. As with my cat-induced insomnia, I sometimes wonder how this frame of mind affects my personality.

"How much have you saved?"

I'm embarrassed to say the number. "About forty thousand dollars."

"What the fuck? You've saved forty thousand dollars?"

"For a rainy day."

I'm paid as a permalancer, or as someone who is less of a mirthless tool might put it, a permanent freelancer. I have an hourly rate and I submit monthly invoices. I was hired under this structure almost two years ago. A year later, after our parent company had repeatedly refused to put me on the payroll and give me health insurance, I took a gamble. I walked into the office of our previous CEO—stuffing my hands in my pockets so she couldn't see them shaking—and told her I would quit unless she doubled my hourly rate.

"Sure," she said, without looking up.

She did it so quickly, with so little apparent cognitive dissonance, that I wished I'd asked for triple.

"Really?" I said.

She shrugged. "It's not my money. I can't make them give you health insurance, but I do control the freelancer budget. We've been underpaying you. Seems fair."

"Thank you," I said, without hiding my shock. "That is fair." I turned to leave.

"Just so you know," she said eerily, "I'm getting out. I can't control what happens after I leave."

"I understand."

I didn't understand. Was she giving me a raise, or inviting me to spend the winter in her haunted hotel? To be safe, I saved. She left a few months later, and the current CEO stepped in.

Lucy beams. "That is—amazing. Listen, let's talk about this. I know you hate work. It shows. You haven't seemed happy for a while. Maybe you should take what you've saved and live on it for a bit before you start looking for another job."

I consider this. "But what will I do with my time?"

"You can work on poems. Maybe go visit Ruth in California. I think it would be good for us."

I don't like the ring of the last part, but I ignore it.

"I have been meaning to read all of *In Search of Lost Time*."

She laughs. "You can't read Proust when you have a job?"

"No one has ever read Proust and been employed at the same time."

"Well, then you can read Proust."

"I'll think about it."

"Lucy's right," Ruth says on the phone. "I think this could be good for you."

"I'm going to feel like an asshole if I'm completely unemployed," I say. "Maybe Will can bring me along for a delivery every now and then."

"Decent idea. But then you'll have to work with Will."

"Our dear friend Will?" I laugh. "What would be so wrong with that?"

"He has weird rituals around work. He's superstitious—you should have seen him when he was starting his dissertation. Wearing the same clothes over and over. Falling asleep the night before meetings with his advisor watching ASMR videos on YouTube of Trekkies using little brushes to clean their action figures. Lord knows what it's like now."

Parable of Vitamin C

The bureaucrat's organizational powers, though legendary to his colleagues, were for his immediate family eclipsed by his curious habit of washing his penis in a glass of freshly squeezed orange juice every morning before heading off, with a friendly wave, to the job at which everyone agreed he excelled.

NOVEMBER

Perhaps being fired would be more dignified if I were to put it in a novel.

Portrait of a Lady is one of my favorite novels. Henry James sometimes makes it difficult to imagine people having physical bodies, but the characters are so vivid. Their psychologies are complex, pliable, adamantine, but they only become real in relation to their surroundings. The characters probe new environments and circumstances like UFOs, using hats and dogs to do the work of perception and communication: she is not wearing a hat upon exiting the house and surveying the great lawn, indicating that she must be staying for a spell; her cousin is of two minds about her—you can tell because his ballistic dog runs up to her in supine eagerness while he unfixes his gaze from the blades of grass in the middle distance and settles in to look at her face, this time for the first time.

Dream, 11/16

The ghost of Henry James is not a human-shaped spirit, but a sound—specifically the purring of a cat on my chest. It is only

Henry James's ghost if the sound is issuing from a cat sitting on my chest. Otherwise the purring is just purring, a part of the room.

HEAVEN JUST GOT ONE HELL OF A FIRE DEPARTMENT reads the faded bumper sticker commemorating the 9/11 dead.

Can we not let them rest?

Parable of Autumn

Ditching work on a Friday, I fly to Houston to visit my grandfather.

His business was air-conditioning. He was a gifted engineer, enjoying local fame in Houston for designing the original cooling system for the Astrodome. Air-conditioning made clear thought possible in a Texas summer seemingly for the first time—it shaped the city. What else would a large-scale interior climate give Houstonians? I remember him telling me how he got the idea—seeing crowds fanning themselves in a line waiting for food, he recognized a problem he could solve. He learned to manipulate the temperature of a large indoor space in which spectators smoked thousands of packs of cigarettes an hour during a ball game. Then he executed his learning. He voted for Barry Goldwater, Richard Nixon, Ronald Reagan, untold numbers of Bushes, and once told me that the greatest threat to American society was unions.

When I was twelve, as we waited to get photos developed in Rite Aid, he and a stranger stood looking at a stock photo of a hot-air balloon. He leaned into her ear and, to my horror, I heard him whisper, "Other than fucking it's the greatest feeling there is." Once he saw me reading *Catch-22* and asked what the book was about. I said it was about war, but that it was funny. A pall came over him. "You shouldn't read that garbage," he said. "Nothing funny about war."

All my other grandparents died before we really knew one another, so maybe I've been warped by some kind of filial Stockholm syndrome. Were we not related, or, God forbid, had he ever been my boss, I would probably despise him. But despite his odious politics, embarrassing public behavior, and stadium-scale carbon footprint, I love him—and what's more, I like him.

When he took me to museums, he would ask me to explain what I liked about a painting, and I would find myself articulating thoughts I didn't know I had. He was the first person to ask me to explain a poem I'd written—to this day I can't explain a poem I've written, probably never will, but it forced me to ask questions of myself that provide the requisite mystery to keep making art that no one else is asking for.

He taught me how to catch and clean a fish. He taught me how to bake bread. He didn't make me feel ashamed when I cried in his presence, as other men of his generation and political persuasion did. He made a deranged quacking sound like a haunted duck when he had an audience of a baby, and the baby always laughed. When he was happy he sang a song that went, "Where the honeysuckle blooms so sweet it durn near makes you sick."

My mom and I meet at the hotel straight from the airport and drive to his house, where he is living with round-the-clock nursing care, for which he wisely set aside funds long ago.

"Dad, this is D__, your grandson," my mom says. "Do you remember him?"

"Who?"

I had expected this, but it still hurts. "Hi, Grandpa."

"Hello!"

"D__ is a poet, remember? Maybe he can read you a poem."

"Oh. Good!"

My mom occasionally does this, asking me to play the part of poet, to interpret a poem she saw in *The New Yorker* that meant nothing to me, or worse, to explain one of my own—and while I recognize that it would be worse still if she never asked at all, it is uncomfortable. It isn't practical or desirable to be a poet in every family situation. But I do my best to play along.

"Sure! Do you want to hear one of my poems, or an old one?"

"Well, yours."

I'm touched, though I know he has no idea what he's asking for, and I don't have a poem that's appropriate for this occasion. It doesn't matter—I read him the one I wrote after Ashbery died.

He shrugs. "You've lost me."

My mom and I burst out laughing.

"How about an older one now?" I say.

"Sure!"

I go to his bookshelf and find the only book of poetry there, an ancient Keats volume. I pull it off the shelf and read him "To Autumn."

He shrugs again. "You've lost me."

My mom and I laugh even harder.

"So you're saying I'm just as good as Keats?"

"Sweet boy," he says. "The greatest feeling there is."

He falls asleep at the table. My mom allows her face to fall to grief.

Dream, 11/18

I finish peeing off the nothing at the end of an unfinished bridge, like the nothing at the end of the Bridge of Avignon. It's snowing. Our blue cat dives after my urine, but instead of falling in the water he hovers over the surface in the snowflakes, blurred, as if he were in a Gerhard Richter painting. His brother, the tabby, stands by me and watches.

A novel is unpaid labor, while poetry is labor's ash.

Parable of Lifting

He held in one arm the certainty of his guilt, and in the other his well-nursed, righteous sense of injury. But despite such a load, his arms, it goes without saying, were never sore.

WINTER NOTEBOOK, 2017/18

DECEMBER

On the first day of the month, almost everyone is fired, finally. Fatima is kept on as a "transitional copywriter." I'm happy for her. I relinquish my laptop and steal a yellow thirteen-inch ruler.

Fatima walks me to the elevator and puts her hand on my shoulder. "It was great working with you," she says. "I hope our paths cross again someday."

Outside, snow is falling heavily, unseasonably early, the flakes dropping like crumpled paper.

A line of cars is buried in smooth white drifts, as if in tribute to the design-forward anal beads we sold.

My grandfather died today.

A card arrives from the CEO—an image of a reindeer carrying a lit menorah. "Thank you for adding some poetic spark to our organization," it reads, "and for the book. Happy holidays."

I throw it in the trash.

Parable of Trash

Your Jesus is not metaphoric, but actual trash. I don't mean this pejoratively. The man you call Jesus just happens to be a bag of garbage: you cast him out, then take him in; his most ardent followers will surely destroy the earth; you can find him virtually anywhere. These are the facts. And this trash's love is real.

For the first month of unemployment, this is all I've written. And let's face it: this is nothing.

JANUARY

Paradise has a limited vocabulary. Hell is more eloquent.

Today my grandfather would have been one hundred. He never cared for music but liked animals. I saw my first horse, hummingbird, fire ant, scorpion with him by my side. He taught me what a barred owl says: "Who cooks for you?"

A blizzard hits New York. Outside the apartment window, snow gathers on the buildings. The entire city is cloaked, affixed with a silencer. There hasn't been this much snow in New York in years. I wonder how many more inches we'll get in my lifetime; snow in New York, as in a poem, is shorthand for borrowed time.

The walls of the apartment begin to shake. I sit bolt upright—an earthquake? A blizzard and an earthquake on the same night. Only in New York. Then, through the wall, a man explosively groans, "Oh. My. God." The room stops shaking, then starts again. Very faintly, someone else says, "I don't think what you're trying to do is anatomically possible, but I'm into it."

The snow falls anatomically. I'm into it.

An inventory of things the unemployed might fruitfully ignore.

The starlight singing from its stump?

The ground nut singing from its nick?

The barred owl singing from its kitchen?

Starlight terminates at the eye. Ground nut terminates at the air. No longer poetry, a photosynthetic process conceals its blossoming meat.

To think that the only thing preventing me from having thoughts like these all day, every day was gainful employment.

In the last three weeks I have entered a state of nearly psychedelic boredom—a mental space like these socks I pack for my grandfather's funeral, soft caves tipped with gold, tunneling into a blackness as deep as midnight, thinner than paper.

In Houston, after the memorial service, Lucy and I return to my grandfather's house with my parents.

"Take this," my mom says, handing me the urn as she steps out of the car, "we're going to take a family picture. Be ready in ten." She slams the door.

The first and only time I have held the entire weight of him in my arms. I remove the lid and study the ash, searching for traces of the person who designed the air-conditioning system for the Astrodome. My dad puts his hand on my shoulder.

"Don't sneeze," he says solemnly.

Extended family and friends are gathered, a chaotic scene. We all collect a few items that we want to save, strewn across several rooms. I pick a shirt, a violin without strings, a handful of photographs.

"Look at this," my dad says, entering the kitchen from the garage holding several saws. "You ever saw so many saws?" He wags his eyebrows.

"Why are you holding those?" my mom says, glaring at him. "Everyone needs to gather for a photo."

"Do you think it would be weird to take this shirt?" I say to Lucy, holding it up to my chest. "I think it fits. The fabric is nice, but I don't want him to, like, haunt me."

She stares at me.

"I think I'm going to take it," I say.

In the corner I notice my great-uncle Isidore, my grandfather's last surviving brother, almost one hundred himself. He is reading Keats, ignoring us.

"We're taking a family picture right now!" My mom stamps her foot in the kitchen, rattling the dishes in the cabinets, and bursts into tears. The house falls silent. Uncle Isidore doesn't look up from his book.

"How are you," I say to Lucy the next day at the airport as we wait to board.

She considers this. "Sometimes it can be hard to want to be a part of your family," she says, squeezing my hand. "But that shirt will look good on you."

After flying home, I use some of the money I have saved to give myself a short writing residency—a room at a bed-and-breakfast in Maine for a week. I drive up to a deep freeze. Every day, when the sun goes down at four p.m., I draw myself a hot bath. This is as close as I get to a creative activity while I'm there—I write nothing.

Parable of Solitude

On my way home, I realize I will be passing by the cabin of an old friend, Eliza, someone whom I have not seen in nearly eight years. I text her to see if she is free, and she invites me over. She will be out when I arrive but says to let myself in.

Eliza and I met in college writing workshops. After graduation, she moved to the woods. A recluse—but a friendly one—she lives by a marsh in an isolated part of the state, without electricity or indoor plumbing. Eight years ago I was driving home from a hiking trip, needed a place to stay for the night on my way, and called. She put me up without hesitation. We took this kind of hospitality for granted with a sprawling range of friends and acquaintances from age twenty-two to twenty-seven, before our lives truly began and we pushed people away, as time grew scarce and the continental drift of age and estrangement set in.

That first visit, it was summer. When I arrived, she was clumsily chopping at a log with a large axe that looked like it had never been used. I was about to go to grad school for poetry, she was doing whatever this was, and I marveled at her isolation and commitment to the bit.

We picked wild blueberries behind her cabin and talked about our writing. Eliza said she had been working on a novel since college, but each time she finished a draft, she reread it, deemed it lacking, threw it away, and started again from scratch.

"You can't be serious," I said. "You don't even save a draft?"

"No point." She grinned. "It keeps the process fresh. If I went back in and messed with it—I know myself. I would smother it. Haven't you ever done that with a poem?"

I thought about it. "Once," I said, "I accidentally deleted a poem and rewrote it from memory."

"And?"

"It was better the second time," I admitted. "But that's a poem—probably less than twenty lines."

"You remembered the parts that were worth remembering and let the parts that weren't interesting slip away."

It got chilly when the sun went down. As I pulled my sleeping bag out of its stuff-sack, she invited me to join her in the bed. I climbed in. She shut out the light. It was pitch-dark.

"Does this seem romantic to you?" she said suddenly. I couldn't see her face.

"It does, actually," I said.

There was a silence.

"People who visit always say that. It makes sense, I guess. But I don't want to confuse you—this is my life. I'm not going anywhere. This isn't going anywhere."

But I was confused. "Why did you invite me into your bed?"

"Because I feel close to you," she said without hesitation, turning her back to me and pressing her body against mine. "But it's not romantic."

Eight years later, a fresh snow has fallen. I park at the end of the icy dirt road, walk through the woods, and enter the cabin, where two logs are smoldering in the stove, over which Eliza has set a pot of chicory tea with a note telling me to help myself to a cup. The floor is frigid; the marsh outside is in some tentative state of thaw. After nearly an hour, an unfamiliar woman enters the cabin. We stare at each other.

"Hi," she says. "Is the tea oversteeped?"

When I do recognize her, I understand a number of things all at once: that I had not remembered her face accurately at all, because her absence from social media is total, and I don't have a photo of her; that in at least eight years, and probably many more, I have not had occasion to truly forget *anyone's* face; that Eliza has aged, as apparently have I; that having forgotten Eliza's face, and only being able to half conjure what I remember of it upon reencountering her in this moment, overlaid with the mask of several years, makes me ecstatically sad. I feel as if I have stepped to the side of time, and yet am more deeply involved in it than I have ever been.

"Hi," I finally manage to say.

"How have you been?"

We talk until dark. Through the window, in the moonlight through the trees, I watch her skillfully heave an axe down through the icy air, effortlessly splitting a large log. She reenters the cabin and throws it in the stove.

"Why have you stayed here for so long?" I say as she rubs her hands together.

She shrugs. "I love it here. It's hard to live like this and I'm good at it. It's not an experience a lot of people get to have, and it seems worth having. It helps with my writing."

"What are you working on these days?"

She grins. “Same novel.”

“Get the fuck out. This is performative.”

“Who am I performing for? You? It will be right when it’s right.”

I roll out my sleeping bag on the floor. She turns out the light.

“It’s really nice to see you, D__,” she says warmly. “I’m glad you came through.”

“You know,” I say, “I almost didn’t recognize you when you walked in earlier. I hadn’t even seen a photo of you for so long. For a second I thought you were a totally different person.”

“Hmm,” she says. The darkness is total, and she sounds serious. “I’m the same.”

Back in Brooklyn, I stare at a photo on my phone of my grandfather holding a pigeon.

Black-and-white, save for the faintest reflection of my own face in the glass. He looks young, probably in his twenties, but could be late teens. Sun leaning hard on his right, slacks perfectly pressed, a strong crease down the leg, and the spackled shadow of a small tree on the side of the house directly to his left. He stands very straight, just off the sidewalk. His posture says he is trying to be still. His hair is neatly shorn, and he is wearing a jacket and a vest. A bolero tie? Hard to say. Most likely just a starched collar. He’s not smiling, but a light puff of baby fat rounds the corners of his mouth, lending him an intensely serious but permanently bemused expression. He has shoved his sense of humor into his gut so it doesn't infiltrate his limbs. A pigeon stands in the palm of his right hand with its neck stretched up, staring hard directly into the light source. Its tail feathers dangle down his hand. His left arm hangs loosely at his side.

I become myself when I describe him; when I imitate him I also become myself. And then the moment passes, and, in both cases, I become someone else.

Dream, 1/31

"Go on, that stream isn't going to stand on itself. Don't fool. I heard it going around you. The greatest feeling there is."

FEBRUARY

A month into my unemployment, I begin reading Proust. *In Search of Lost Time*: a book that takes so long to read, you cannot help but be changed in the interval. But changed how?

Lucy is seated on the couch next to me, watching a movie on her computer. I tap her on the shoulder. She removes her earbuds.

"When I'm done reading Proust, will you tell me how I've changed?" I say. "I'm worried I won't notice it happening."

She looks at the floor. "Sure," she says flatly, "I'm on the case," and reinserts her earbuds.

I open the first page of *Swann's Way*.

Parable of the Party

Will and I are seated on a couch in the corner of the office of a literary magazine, an issue launch party. A man in tailored beige clown pants and a faded black hoodie with no shirt underneath sits down next to us and lights a cigarette.

“Can I bum one?” says Will.

“These are Aesops,” he says, pulling a cigarette out of a small gold paper box. “You’ll taste the difference.”

“The luxury soap company? They make cigarettes?”

“They’re limited edition.”

“I want to taste the difference too,” I say. “Can I bum one?”

“You can share. Are you writers?”

“We’re poets,” says Will. “But my real passion is delivering office furniture.”

“I’m currently unemployed,” I say. “I’ve been reading Proust.”

“I’m hearing and loving that,” clown pants hoodie says. “What is your poetry about?”

“Most of it doesn’t rhyme.”

“Lately I’ve been really into medieval allegory and penitence,” Will says. “Are you a writer?”

“I’m a journalistic language sculptor.”

"This cigarette really is delicious," Will says, passing it to me. I take a drag. It's like charcoal and cucumber. "But what does it mean, the thing you just said?"

"I just got back from Stuttgart. Every day while I was there I trekked into the forest outside the city to masturbate into spiderwebs."

"Wow," I say, "I've heard about that fellowship." I really had. "Congratulations."

He nods once.

"Sorry if I'm misunderstanding," Will says. "I thought you said you sculpt language?"

"Cum is speech, is it not?" he says, craning his neck around us and beckoning someone over. "The etymological root of semen is 'seed,' did you know that? To sow. And the spiderweb is the most non-fictional structure in nature. My father is Jewish and my maternal grandmother was bitten by a German shepherd on a ski trip in the Alps not long after the Berlin Wall fell. So I carry a certain amount of history and trauma. By releasing my seed onto the 'webs'"—he makes scare quotes in the air with his fingers, which is confusing, as he is referring to literal spiderwebs—"I hope to elucidate the roots of European fascism. That's me. Who do you know here?"

"No one. We heard about the party from the internet," I say. "Both of my parents are Jewish," I add, for some reason.

"It's cold and this is the only place in New York where you can smoke indoors," Will says.

Someone's hand emerges through the throng of partygoers, directly in front of clown pants' face, holding a key with a healthy bump of white powder on the end of it. He looks up with great concern, his brow furrowed, eyes darting between us.

"Is your cocaine gluten free?" A small nitrous canister clatters to the floor a few feet away.

"That's not my hand," I say. I raise my hands in the air to show him. Will does the same.

"You two are amazing," he says, the powder spirited away up his nose. The hand disappears back into the crowd. "'That's not my hand.' You really are poets."

My contemporaries, white and gelatinous—ambulatory piles of gefilte fish granted wit and the power of speech.

I am reading *Swann's Way* in my underwear when Lucy gets home from work. She looks exhausted.

"Listen to this," I say. "'Between the flowers and the blackened stone against which they leaned, if my eyes perceived no interval, my mind reserved an abyss.' Isn't that an incredible sentence?"

"Wow," Lucy says, using a tissue to pick up a damp hair ball I have neglected since the blue cat coughed it up that afternoon. "Listen, we're about to close an issue at work. I'm wrecked. Can you tell me what you want from the Thai place if you're not going to cook?"

"Drunken noodles, thanks. When this is over and I get another job—do you think we'll call it an interval, or an abyss?"

"I think that's for you to decide."

Love is not aleatory, but a certain strain of atmospheric disturbance literally is.

"Did I tell you I ran into Chester at the farmer's market?" Ruth says on the phone.

"Chester from poetry school? U BE PUBE Chester?"

"Yes! He was carrying a bag of squash. We're getting a drink this week. It'll be interesting to find out . . . what kind of squash he has in his bag. Know what I mean?"

"Yes, unfortunately, you're coming through loud and clear."

"I'm referring to his di—"

"Yep, got it. I always liked that guy."

"He's not a poet anymore—he works for Apple and plays drone clarinet in an avant-garde jazz collective."

"Drone clarinet?"

"That's how he described it. I listened on Spotify. It's better than it sounds."

"I believe you. The fact that he works for Apple is a little more disturbing."

"Whatever. At least he has his shit together. I'm not fucking around anymore. I'm only dating people who are serious about building a future and respect my art like they would respect anyone else's career. They should have a good job, they should at least read Creeley, they should be willing to put me on their health insurance if we're having unprotected sex, and if they don't text me back within forty-five minutes, that's gaslighting. Two hours if it's in the middle of the night."

"A former poet who works in tech and makes music on the side—this dude might actually fit the bill."

"He's five-eleven—only a couple of inches taller than me. I don't know."

"Very curious to hear how this date goes."

"What about you? How are things with Lucy?"

"I think we might be in a bit of a rut. My joblessness is wearing on her. We aren't really—I'm spending the night on the couch a lot. Everyone around us is evolving in their lives and we're staying the same."

"Wherever you two are going, I know that you will locate yourselves there."

"How long have you sounded like you live in LA?"

"I'm serious. Time changes us so incrementally that we don't realize it as it's happening. Everything has a schedule, if you can find out what it is."

Will texts that he has a job next week moving some furniture into a new building in Manhattan and asks if I want to ride along and help him. He can give me a couple hundred dollars in cash.

Dream, 2/27

A lion who speaks to me without his teeth puts them back in and speaks more clearly.

You can swallow all the words you like, but they remain inedible.

SPRING NOTEBOOK, 2018

MARCH

If you listen carefully, you'll notice that the subway is in three-part harmony with itself—but beware the train singing with three voices. It takes you nowhere.

Luckily, I'm no longer a commuter.

Even the subway emergency contact system contains its own poetry.

> TO TALK
> PRESS, RELEASE
> AND WAIT FOR
> STEADY LIGHT

Nice enjambment. But how long will we have to wait while this woman's pant leg is caught in the sliding door of the underworld?

"Help! Please, help! My cuff hath been tugged by Gravity's lap-dog!"

In the used/new bookstore, on the spine of the used copy of *The Diary of Vaslav Nijinsky*, for some reason the word "diary" is crossed out.

Parable of the Convex Mirror

Will and I pull up to the Lower Manhattan office building at eight p.m. with a van full of furniture.

"Is this stuff beautiful or garbage?" I say as Will opens the back of the van to reveal a geometric stack of gray and beige angles. "I honestly can't tell."

Is it even furniture? Verifiably, it is flat planks of metal, wood, and cloth affixed with legs—on which someone could conceivably sit or place smaller objects—inspired by true tables and chairs, to be sure. But are these objects actually spectral ornaments, furniture's ex machina, the 3D-printed ghosts of the furniture machine?

"That's the principle of office furniture," Will says, counting the pieces in the back of the van. "To make employees feel wealthy and degraded at the same time. In any case, it's expensive, so be careful with it—shit, there are thirteen."

"Is that a problem?"

"It's—fine. Just one short of sonnet. Fourteen is good luck."

"Is this one of your little work rituals, counting furniture?"

"I'm a formalist."

We pull a heavy coffee table out of the van. Lifting with our knees, we carry it in small gliding steps, with sylphic smoothness, into the service elevator.

"Make it quick, guys," the building manager says. "Trying to get home soon."

The doors open to a gleaming hallway divided from the office by a glass wall. The open floor plan inside discloses a system of conference rooms and smaller executive offices, also made of glass. I balance the coffee table on my leg as I open the door. We bend our knees to gently place it on the ground.

"Nicely done," says Will.

We unload all the furniture until there is only one object left—a mesmerizing reflective orb, gleaming like a pumpkin-scale drop of mercury at the back of the van. It isn't particularly heavy, but unwieldy enough that Will and I need to carry it together.

We whisk it off the service elevator, moving quickly and efficiently with the light load. I stare into it, caught in its convex reflection—our hands and torsos enormous in its silvery edifice, the office lights gleaming and curving over its globular surface like a meteor shower slipping through our crescent-shaped heads as we walk down the hall.

"You're not bad at this," Will says as we approach the office door. "Maybe we just discovered your hidden talent."

"I don't have any hidden talents. They're all right here on the surface."

"Surface is just visible core. Watch your—"

At that moment, my back smashes into the glass door. It shatters into a hundred thousand pieces.

We stare at one another, holding the mirrored orb, an alarm blaring through the building and strobe lights flashing in the shards of glass.

The next day I text Will an apology.

> Did I do it deleterious, to have me be so dumb?

A pretty good line, I think—contrite, sincere, syntactically interesting. Will loves this kind of thing. But weirdly, he doesn't reply.

In the end, he isn't fired, but he is responsible—he finally texts to tell me, a few days later—for replacing the glass door. I forfeit my cut of the delivery, of course, and dip a few hundred dollars further into my savings to split it with him.

He won't stay mad at me. But it's safe to say that my office furniture delivery career is over.

Dream, 3/16

As if bewitched by the sound, I stalk little melodies through a manor. I find a cat rusting inside a baby grand piano. When his ears twitch, bits of metal flake off and flutter through the strings. He looks at me and blinks, brushes his tail against a C, stretches his paw and hits E minor, plucks a D with his claws. I understand that just as I visit a doctor, this cat is being medicated by this music.

Cats. Imagine. To reject labor external to the self. To tongue-bathe oneself in a court of law.

As a poet, I feel beautifully useful—but only by a clean window when it's snowing.

Snow: an adverb about to end.

Usefulness: a genre distinct from labor.

Beauty: see above. A wrecking ball.

Cleanliness: after godliness. Poets erroneously call it "clarity."

Windows: an adverb bracing for impact.

Godliness: a court of law.

Today's Lucy's and my seventh anniversary.

There are some things I keep to myself out of sadness, and some out of a happiness so total I have trouble seeing it for what it is.

Seven Years

Dumb blossoms reply to the poem
"Whoso List to Hunt" or whatever the hell
All I know about sun is that it
Makes my mask unmanageable

"Whoso List to Hunt" or whatever the hell
Remembers me to my mother tongue's mud and
Makes my mask unmanageable
With another word for this face I rent

Remembers me to my mother tongue's mud and
Like a movie erased and not to be repeated
With another word for this face I rent
I enter seven digits and call the number

Like a movie erased when the lights go up
Here you are then
I enter seven digits and call the number
Number by number, D-A-F-F-O-D-I-L

Here you are then
Here's the constellations
Number by number, D-A-F-F-O-D-I-L
Including, yeah, the extra number

Hears the constellations
And you closed your book to listen too
Including, yeah, the extra number
No one but you had heretofore heard

And you closed your book to listen to
Dumb blossoms reply to the poem
No one but you had heretofore heard
All I know about sun is that it

APRIL

Parable of Two Shepherds

Two shepherds approach the crest of a hill. One of them has been inconvenienced, and is enraged. His gaze sweeps the valley as he intones, "I'll stab the clouds with my horns!"

The other stands back and looks at his companion; not only at him, but at all of him.

"Jesus, those are your *real* horns?"

In a pantoum, the second and fourth lines from the opening quatrain become the first and third lines of the following stanza, forming the fertilized ground in which two brand-new lines take root. This pattern can be repeated ad infinitum, until the first and third lines of the opening stanza circle back to end the poem.

A couple in a long relationship learns within four or five years that the only rule of repetition is difference. You laugh at the same jokes, you have the same fight, you wake up next to the same body, but time makes its nearly imperceptible alterations. Just as you settle into your life with someone, you realize that your life has changed. Seven years into a relationship, these changes become the unbendable rule.

When I give Lucy the pantoum I wrote for her, she throws her arms around me and plants a kiss on my ear, thrillingly missing my cheek. She puts it in the book she is reading and then—I know her well—forgets. I have learned to cherish this, to wait for the day years later when she will open the book, the unexpected relic fluttering out to be discovered anew.

"The time we have at our disposal every day is elastic, the passions we feel expand it, those that we inspire contract it, and habit fills up what remains." (Proust, *Within a Budding Grove*)

Dream, 4/8

"Beautiful eyes. Have you always had them?"

Parable of Two Ringtones

Two ringtones singing to one another in a dark movie theater.

The first ringtone hides in the hills and repeats anything the second ringtone says.

The second ringtone is so in love with its own voice that upon hearing this it leans in, then falls with a splash and drowns in a pool of sound.

I am working in a café. A generational malady: luminescent white apple hovering just above our laps at every table, an apple we have obsequiously accepted into our red cloaks from the wolfish hand of grandmother gig economy. I am no exception. If email smelled like whoever sent it, I think, we would send less. A form of writing that is almost entirely divorced from the body. I check mine, which contains—not surprisingly, because I have not submitted any applications, but disappointingly nonetheless—no job offers.

A gremlin-like wail erupts from the other end of the room. I look up and lock eyes with a woman my age, across the table. She smiles. I panic. I was good at flirting once, but the skill has atrophied.

"No way that sound is coming out of a real baby, right?" I say, laughing nervously and cracking my knuckles. Her eyes quickly fall back to her screen.

The furtive glance is my Odette. Email is my Albertine.

Notebooks are more private than poetry, but barely. A performance for an audience of one. Or perhaps they are transcripts of the silent conversations that pass between two strangers in public. An eloquent eye contact between the present and the future.

Privacy, a public value.

Today's my birthday. Lucy and I go to our favorite pizza place. We read silently as we eat, which I tell myself isn't depressing because we like reading together. There at the table, as I turn thirty-three, my Jesus year, I think about Proust's description of Odette's clothing: a technological finery near the edge of civilization. Lucy and I have not dressed up for this occasion but age itself is its own garment, and for Jesus the age of thirty-three was as close to the edge of civilization as he got.

Older, slower, sadder, more cognitively obtuse, and better than ever.

Be still and let your eyes adjust to the subtler tones of its motion and you will see, from across blushed desert vistas or from the cramped bough of a restaurant awning under which your waiter is catching the manna of his smoke break, the tender, almost bashful way rain hides the fact that it always falls the way of hell.

Ever the seeker of fresh discovery, I opted not to pay quarterly taxes in the last year, even though I was, temporarily, a permalancer—better to calculate and submit my patronage to American empire in one thrilling deposit rather than mete it out in tightly controlled dribs and drabs.

The danger of expecting the unexpected, as we know, is that surprise becomes rote. But when I calculate and recalculate what I owe to the state of New York and the US government, I see that

I needn't have worried about this. Looking at this figure is like encountering *The Waste Land* for the first time, or a craft hovering over you on a deserted road as it pulls you up a beam of light. An almost Wagnerian sum of money—artful and shocking.

Since December, I have budgeted my forty-thousand-dollar savings to last through the summer, perhaps the year. Living frugally but comfortably, just over nine thousand remains after taxes. Not a death blow, but certainly death-blowish. My mini retirement will need to end a bit sooner than I'd hoped.

Dream, 4/20

Ruth explains that her spices are her cats.

"See?" she says, framing the spice rack with her hands in an equal sign. "These are *my* cats."

Imagine a poem that describes something by describing what it's not. Shakespeare did this in a sonnet beginning "My mistress' eyes are nothing like the sun." Bashō's poetry somehow spells out what's gone in the names of the people and places he encounters.

Unlike Bashō

No Black Hair Mountain.
No change of clothes.
No young girl named Double.

No friend from whom I've stolen poems.
No horse sent back with money in its saddle.
No house called "Death Barrier."
No "life-taking stones."
No mirrors, no meter.
No feet, no sneakers.
No people, no plants, no heat, no speaker.

Lucy sits down next to me on the couch as I'm reading Proust.

"I think we have to talk," she says, bursting into tears.

"All I want to do," I say to Ruth on the phone, "is get in my car and drive across the country and floor it directly into the Pacific Ocean."

"You two have been together a long time. I don't think this is the wrong decision."

"It would be like a silent yoga retreat," I continue, "except instead of someone telling me to torture myself in a gentle voice, I could watch the landscape change and then die."

"When are you moving out?"

"I'm not sure. Neither of us are in a rush—I'm going to go stay with my parents for a while, then when I get a job I'll find my own place."

"Listen to me. Do not draw this out and make it as painful as possible. Make it clean."

"You sound like a mob boss."

"How's Lucy doing?"

"She's sad. We're both very sad. The cats seem fine though."

"You know, my coursework ends next month. What if I fly out east at the beginning of July, then you drive me back to the Bay? Road trip! Maybe we could even set up some readings along the way. And you could get to know Chester better and meet Homer."

"Homer?"

"The stray cat Chester and I have taken in."

"I didn't realize you guys were already at the cat adoption phase."

"He's really wonderful."

I am silent.

"Love you both," she continues. "Let me know if you need anything. I'll book my ticket tomorrow."

Parable of Masks

She took good care of her masks. For example, each of her masks had its own mask, and she went to great lengths to ensure that each of these masks of masks themselves had a fine set of masks of their own. But there her generosity ended.

MAY

I've long had the fantasy of knowing something without learning it. I have this fantasy because it actually happened to me when I first met Lucy.

Will introduced us in the library when we were in grad school—they had been in a seminar together. I was shocked by how beautiful she was. Her face like handwriting. It took a moment to decipher its intricacies, its elegantly messy shorthand and the complexities of its motion, but before long I learned how to read it, an extension of her actual syntax. On our first date, we were walking through a graveyard on the edge of town. She said, "I think his beard, Bob Ross's, might for me be, like, part of his voice?" Later, when I read her poetry, I recognized the style.

"I think I'm going to teach that sentence to my poetry students."

"Your students are lucky."

"To hear sentences transmitted from Mars to your mouth in a college classroom? I agree."

"That they get to look at you for two and a half hours every week."

The sky above us turned to green brain coral. It was about to rain hard, but we had stopped walking. We regarded each other for a moment. She nodded at the graves without breaking eye contact. "I think they want us to move."

As she said this her expression changed, or perhaps mine did, and then hers. It was as if we had each suddenly taken a bruise behind both eyes—simultaneously punched by the nimble, well-moisturized, invisible fist of an angel.

We dissolved in one another's presence like this for seven years. But none of this constituted knowing something without learning it. What I knew without learning it was that Lucy and I had already met, though we had not, and would continue knowing one another for a long time.

That reality is like a radio signal fading out as you drive into the mountains. You can continue to hum the song to yourself. You know it well. But it's not the same.

Dream, 5/3

My Social Security number in front of a black background with the five blinking back and forth to four.

Lucy and I achieve an uneasy equilibrium. I sleep on the couch.

The signal is clearer when we don't talk—as it has been, I realize in retrospect, for months.

Parable of the Botanical Garden

In the public garden: people walking and fixing their hair, creeping up to tulips, women close-talking, a German man nearly wet-nursing his phone, saying "Da" into it.

In the public garden: something there is that doesn't love a wall of undead daffodils.

Nevertheless, despite their baggage, the landscapists take their waters to them.

A joy that I am not experiencing firsthand nonetheless orders me to wave my limbs.

Specifically, this joy orders me to put my hands in the air.

Then to wave them like I just don't care.

Parable of Grammar

"I prefer grammar."

"To my poem?"

"Yes, but also to the subject of your poem."

"You prefer grammar as a concept?"

"No. As an experience."

Orpheus steals and redistributes dirty money from the air. The flowers lean in to listen.

These notes I take are yours.

I come back from an evening walk. The days are getting longer, bleeding into night. Tonight the light is a dull lilac, the apartment is hot, aquatic, quiet. I open the bathroom door. Lucy is there in a steaming bath.

"Hi."

"Can I come in and sit with you?"

"Sure."

I lean on the sink and roll myself a joint.

"You look cool when you do that," she says.

I look down at her in the water, her hair damp and her face flushed. She is smiling.

"Oh? What else do I look cool doing?"

"Not much. Better not lose the skill set."

I light the joint and pass it to her. "What will you do here when I'm gone?"

"No idea. Maybe I'll finally read *Middlemarch*."

"Bullshit. You're going to watch Fred and Ginger movies on a loop while the cats fight over which one gets to sleep directly on your face."

She laughs. "Do you want to get in the tub?"

I give her a look.

"We both know we're not going to have sex," she says. "But it would be nice to be close."

I slip into the bath opposite her, the faucet lodged on my shoulder like a silver parrot. We slouch together awkwardly, knee to knee, then ease into the touch. The water is more than warm, less than hot. The cats watch us from the toilet lid.

"We never took baths together," I say. "Why?"

"We didn't have to. The whole seven years has been a bath." She hits the joint forcefully.

"I wouldn't take a day of it back," I say.

"Me ne—" Lucy begins to say before a massive belch shoves the word aside, ricocheting across the tile, the terrified cats bolting into the hall. A ribbon of smoke curls from her mouth.

As we both laugh harder than we have in months, I know—without learning it—that I will remember this moment and relive it in variation, a holy meme, for the rest of my life.

Lucy is a heroic sleeper. It's an art for her. When she turns out the light, she's instantly elsewhere. Her dreams, when she shared them with me, were masterpieces of narrative gradient, crystalline figuration, and logical drift, not unlike her poems. I sleep lightly by comparison.

The cats wake me in the middle of the night. The blue one cries out from the other room—his memory is short, and in the hours before dawn he often becomes frantic that we have left him. My heart breaks at the sound. The tabby sits and watches him silently, purring. I get out of bed and sit with him sometimes until he quiets down, staring at the glowing red hands on the clock tower as they slowly spin.

I rub the fur behind his ears, telling him that we are here, that we care for him, love him even, that we will feed him in the morning and let him speak through our poems if that's what he wants, if he will only let me sleep. But he seems to not know what he wants, though the desire itself is powerful and vivid to him, and he never remembers what I say.

I return to bed. Lucy doesn't stir.

I look at her, dreaming deeply, and wonder what she is seeing in this moment.

I close my eyes and open them.

Parable of Memes

A shimmering vault of memes, familiar as the songs of the ancients but miraculously fresh as a cool mountain stream, bathed its celestial rain down upon each and every one of their earthly deeds.

SUMMER NOTEBOOK, 2018

JUNE

Orpheus tried to perform another song, but a thick cloud of flies kept muting the strings of his lyre.

The sound of the wind rustling the leaves in the part of the country from which I hail eerily resembles the opening chords of the song "Do It Again," by Steely Dan.

On a walk with my mom and my parents' dog at the local nature preserve in the suburb where I grew up. I am in a foul mood, incongruous with how beautiful it is this time of year—a deep green, flowers everywhere. Plants are so self-referential, I think to myself, bitterly. I am staying here while I sort out a new apartment in Brooklyn. The droopy-eyed, empathic yellow lab nuzzles and licks my hand as we walk.

"Our society is so divided," my mom says, furrowing her brow and sipping her half-caf iced coffee, "but I think we can all agree that nature is amazing. Even the people who are cutting down the trees and poisoning the drinking water. They can't feel good about it—who could feel good about that? Not even the worst person in the world. Still, it does make me wish I could really believe in hell, so I could know there was a place for them. Flowers—I mean, are you kidding? They're like witchcraft! In a *good* way!"

At dinner—rainbow trout, sugar snap peas, roasted potatoes with dill, exquisitely prepared by my mom—the empathic dog rests his head on my foot. I haven't said much lately. My dad has his binoculars out, transfixed by the hummingbird at the feeder out the window.

"Look at that hummingbird out there hovering around my feeder, just *sucking* on it," he says.

"Remind me again when Ruth is coming out here for your road trip?" my mom says.

"Beginning of next month," I say through a mouthful of potatoes.

"That will be so fun. I'm glad you'll be able to do that together. She's so great."

"She's like a sister to me and she has a boyfriend."

"I wasn't suggesting anything! Anyway, when do you think you'll start applying for jobs?"

"I guess you'll find out when I do," I snap. We eat in silence for a while. My parents have dutifully not asked me about the breakup, a heroic effort of restraint and respect for my boundaries.

"I'm sorry," I say. "I'm really grateful to you both. I do know that I need to get a job and my own place." I pause. "I think I'm just grieving."

My dad puts the binoculars down.

My mom puts her hand on mine. "That makes a lot of sense," she says. I feel like I might weep.

My dad's eyes go wide. He proceeds carefully. "Grieving. Huh. Grieving. So—sorry, help me out here for a second. You know me. I'm slow. I'm not as good with words as you are."

"It's fine," I say. "Go ahead. You can ask me about it."

He looks worried.

"I think I missed something. Who died?"

Parable of Mozart

Smoking a joint on the driveway and listening to the Jupiter Symphony on my phone speaker at the lowest possible volume, I notice something like laughter in the third movement. An incredible sound—a frothing, desperate happiness, nearly indistinguishable from rage. The neighbor across the street slams his window shut.

When Mozart runs through a dark wood, the only root that can trip him is square.

I've been watching *The Sopranos* for the first time. I read a literary critic's skeptical take: that the show is merely asking whether a sociopath can be a good person. It's a bad-faith reading by someone who hates the medium. Not interesting. *The Sopranos* isn't about that.

It's about what happens to the rest of the world—not you—when you die: it goes on. And it's persuasive.

I notice tonight that I am reflexively, unconsciously checking my pulse.

Dream, 6/15

"Sometimes I just sit with a petri dish and wait a week."

During a speech, the president says, "What you're seeing and what you're reading is not what's happening." The crowd goes wild. We see it replayed on the news.

"We're not even living in a democracy anymore," my mom sighs, flipping the channel.

"Sometimes I think he *wants* to be assassinated," my dad says quietly, his spoon clinking in a bowl of ice cream. "If I had sons like his, I know I would. Mom and I are lucky in that way. We appreciate our lives. We're glad to have this time with you. We'd never want to be assassinated."

"Never say never," my mom says. "But we do love you."

"More than you can imagine."

I throw them a bone and smile a little. They could try less, but they are trying.

My mom settles on a new stand-up special by a very rich, very famous comedian of their generation. This comedian is talking about how much he enjoys baseball—even though, when you think about it, the food at baseball games isn't very good. It isn't very good at all. My parents are both beside themselves.

"That's true!" my dad says, red-faced, wiping tears from his eyes. "That's just true!"

It is horribly clear that I need to start looking for a job. I open LinkedIn, a website whose founders should face trial at the Hague. A copywriting job is listed at a storied Midtown Jewish arts and community center. It doesn't require a cover letter, so I apply.

The next day, I am shocked to receive an email inviting me to come in for an interview.

"Of course," I say in the interview, in a light blue shirt and new gray blazer I bought that morning on my way out of the subway station, because my old one is at my old apartment with Lucy, "my preferred method of writing is collaborative." I don't mention that I'm about to skip town for a few weeks.

"That's good," my interviewer says, "because for this position, collaboration is essential."

It's important to remember that Satan is everywhere. Like poetry, he can take any form at any time, which is why poets are obsessed with him. Whenever I look at the ocean it's hard to forget that in *Paradise Lost*, Satan first came to Earth dressed not as a snake, but as a cormorant—much like the one sitting out under the Brooklyn Bridge, creepily staring at me with its greasy little wings outstretched right now as I write this.

After a couple of weeks in the suburbs, Brooklyn has never looked so beautiful. I don't want to take the train back, even for the night—I have half a mind to just write a check and sleep on the floor of the first apartment Will and I visit today. The wind whips off the harbor and he claps his hand on his head to stop his dirty white baseball cap, emblazoned with SAPPHO in bright red lettering, from blowing away. He takes a swig of coffee and slaps me on the back. "Ready to find the next shithole to rest your bones in?"

A phalanx of nasturtium blossoms strums the rat's belly as it scampers through the city horticulturalist's handiwork. A fine mist settles over the East River.

I think at some point Satan also shows up as a fine mist.

Will and I enter a small, street-level apartment with the building's super. Across the entire living room and kitchen, the floor is covered with a confetti of tiny dead cockroaches.

"This is a nice place," the super says. He knocks on the metal door. "Could stop a bullet."

"I like the layout and the light," I say, not wanting to burn any bridges with this man.

"It seems like there might be a roach problem in the building?" Will says. On the one hand, Will is here to be my advocate, but on the other, he has less skin in the game.

"What do you mean?" the super says.

"There are roaches all over the floor," Will says.

The super glares at us. "Where? Show me where."

"I don't see them," I say.

"Here, for example." Will points at the ground. "Here. Here. Here. Here. All over the kitchen."

"Oh! Well." The super bursts out laughing, then regains a business-like composure. "Those are dead."

"I'm waiting to hear back about a job," I say. "Can I think about it and let you know?"

"I wouldn't wait," the super says. "This place is in high demand. Three people have come to look at it in the last six months."

It is late when I get home, but still not dark. I walk home from the commuter train station in a dusky blue light—the longest day of the year. I pass a house with a flag bearing the silhouette of an AK-47. A couple sits in Adirondack chairs on an impeccably manicured lawn, a lawn like every other in the neighborhood, full of sprawling houses whose cupboards are fully stocked with jar after jar of organic kalamata olives and box after box of Kashi GoLean Crunch. They hold large, dewy glasses of white wine.

Parable of the Fool

"He looks like a fool. He acts like a fool. He speaks of nothing but murder and carnage. He must be a man of the people. And as a man of the people, he has my vote," the count gurgled into his chin, his monocle falling into his chardonnay spritz with a fizzy plop.

"And yet there's something," the countess countered, "quite *lordly* about the pinkness of the skin that rings his eyes, the way he sniffs the earth and licks his cloven foot—don't you think? But in the end, who can say who a man is? It's a mystery." Several seconds passed. She fanned herself.

"It's a mystery," she said again.

Let there be commerce between us.

What if a poem were a kind of voting—voting for the world you want? My votes in the suburbs: the cardinals, the brook behind the school, the spider crawling up the stop sign, a burning cop car, the little alphabet of dew written on the fern. My votes in the city: the starlings, the trains, a burning cop car, the rats running through the walls.

Two years ago, when the president lost the popular vote but won the election, many of us took bitter solace in the anomaly. In a democracy such as ours, we told ourselves—because it was *normal* for democracy to be messy—a popular election occasionally results in a tiny bit of minority rule. And just as a democratic system under minority rule could not reflect poorly on the majority, because minority rule was an anomaly, the president himself could in no way reflect poorly on those who voted against him. Our democracy: *normal.* The president: *not normal.*

But by now it is clear that minority rule is doing its work. When the president signs an executive order this week ending the practice of separating migrant children from their families in de facto prison camps at the border—because he "didn't like the sight or the feeling of families being separated"—is this a sign of the normal triumphing over the not normal?

Separate prisons for children and parents: *not normal.* Families in prison together, under one roof: not quite *normal,* but surely better than *not normal.*

Dream, 6/28

Swimming my way back to shore on a piece of machinery or driftwood with the empathic dog, as at the end of *Jaws.* "That's right, you beautiful bastard, we did it," I say to him in a Richard Dreyfuss voice as he paddles beside me. He is smiling but looks tired.

Parable of the Tick

Tonight I see what looks to be a tick on the dog's eyelid. I get a pair of tweezers from the bathroom and kneel to remove it. He looks at me askance but lies there in beatific patience. I smooth the fine yellow fur on his head, apply the tweezers to the tick, and clamp down. But it is not a tick—just a little black growth above his eye. A stream of blood trickles down his snout, and he doesn't flinch. I gasp. He leans forward and licks my hand, to forgive me for hurting him, with blood in his fur. I burst into tears.

Love is hell.

Parable of AJ Soprano

After unsuccessfully attempting suicide by tying a cinder block to his feet and throwing himself into the family pool—the prelude to perhaps the most piercingly moving scene of the entire series—AJ is still, with a persistence approaching the divine, a complete asshole.

The fly on the engraved hand mirror on the table in the hall—wings on the glass, legs in the air, hanging from its own reflection—sleeping, or spoiled?

JULY

Parable of Ruins

"Maybe when we get to Arkansas we can go to Crystal Bridges. I've always wanted to see it. Supposedly they have an amazing permanent collection."

"I hate museums," I sigh. "What does that even mean, 'permanent collection'? Nothing's permanent."

We are on a bench on the Coney Island boardwalk at sunset. A gorgeous evening, the air steamy and inviting, the Wonder Wheel spinning behind us, throngs of laughing teenagers and families streaming around us, the ocean sprawled out like a boundless pane of glass, a shitty attitude radiating off me like heat. The car is packed and ready to go. We've driven here first, and when we reach LA, we will drive directly to the beach—coast to coast. Ruth's idea. Ritual, she claims, is important during a time of upheaval.

"You don't hate museums," she instructs, trying to make a gentle chiropractic adjustment to the mood of the person with whom she will be spending a great deal of time in an enclosed space in the coming weeks.

"Yes I do!"

"I'm sorry, but you don't. You're a poet. What do you like if you hate museums?"

A thin roseate solar emanation ricochets through the clouds and dapples Ruth's tranquil face as she waits for me to answer. The sky is turning a luminescent purple. The carnival lights pop on. I speak quietly.

"I like ruins."

She nods. "Shut the fuck up and go get in the car."

Our road trip will take us to Baltimore, St. Louis, down through the Arkansas Ozarks, out through the Texas Panhandle, across the Southwest, and into LA. I've packed a tent for when we get to Arkansas, where we will do at least a couple of nights of camping.

One perk of being a poet is that you can give a reading just about anywhere. People love the idea of poetry—the only problem is that most of them don't actually want to read or hear it. It isn't a terrible problem. You won't be paid a dime and no one will listen to a word you say, but it is a good excuse to travel, and you can write it all off as a work expense on your taxes. We're only doing readings at the first two stops—so if anyone gets audited, we can say it's a tour. Two of anything makes a pattern.

"What's the first thing you want to do now that you're untethered?" Ruth says on the way down to Baltimore.

"I guess I'm doing it. I love driving for hours and zoning out on the road. It's like meditation for me."

"You could actually meditate, you know."

"I prefer dumping carbon out of this Subaru as it rolls across the country. Developing the personality of a guy who takes up meditation after a breakup seems like a more convoluted way of poisoning the air. Have you been meditating in LA?"

"No, I've just been fucking a lot."

"So things are going well with Chester?"

"I think the orgasms I've been having are clearing up my skin," she says, using her phone as a mirror. "But I don't know if it has anything to do with Chester, actually—just a moment in my life. Maybe it has something to do with taking Homer in—he looked so sickly when we found him, and now he's fine. I don't know what it is. I feel weirdly at peace with fate."

"Do you like his music?"

She chews for a long time on what must be an extremely dry piece of beef jerky.

"Yes," she says, swallowing.

We pull up to Baltimore at midnight.

Baltimore has a wonderful puking culture. Walking around the harbor after breakfast, Ruth lets it rip right into the water in broad daylight, and everyone walks by her in the late morning sunshine like it's nothing. They seem to be used to this kind of thing. A place where you can be yourself.

"I think I ate too much jerky," Ruth says, spitting.

After a day at the aquarium and perusing bookshops, we do our reading at a nearly empty coffee shop while the barista is cleaning up. Only one guy shows up, but it doesn't matter. My reading is fine. Ruth, as always, is exceptional.

"Very good job up there," the sole attendee says to Ruth, ignoring me. "Are you in grad school?"

"I'm getting my PhD in LA, but in English, not creative writing—"

"I'm at Hopkins. Your poems are very skillful. I did enjoy some of them. You're clearly a real writer. But you haven't fully come into your skills yet. I think the poems would be more resonant if you were taking on the most important themes."

"Interesting!" Ruth says brightly, full of loathing. "Tell me—what are the most important themes?"

"War and ecology. Have you ever killed a deer or man with your car? Human beings are powerful creatures—monstrously powerful—but that power, there's a price to pay for it. Things like that. Things of that nature. Have a nice evening."

He leaves.

Parable of Song

"Interesting song. You must be an academic. Where do you teach?"

"Thank you so much. I'm an assistant professor in the Cryptobio-musicology Department at Garbage College."

In St. Louis, we read between sets at a basement show, before a math rock band called Glass Cornhole. One guy listens to us while everyone else gathers in the back to get beer.

I finish and walk directly from the mic to the beer line. He follows. "Great shit," he congratulates.

"Thanks, man. Thanks for coming out. So—what's the poetry scene like in St. Louis?" His expression changes. Instantly, I know I have said the wrong thing.

"I actually don't draw those kinds of distinctions, between what poetry is and isn't?" he says. "I don't really think that's for me to say? Who am I to say what a poem is, much less a 'scene.' Are you saying that this conversation isn't a 'poetry scene'? Isn't every moment a poem?"

"No, totally," I say. "That's a great point. But—and this is kind of an important question for me right now, actually—what do you think makes poetry different from the conversation that we're having right now? Or any other experience? I kind of need to know. It's been a weird time."

He considers this, skeptically. The guitarist of Glass Cornhole starts beating her instrument with a furry hammer, and feedback fills the basement in waves of eardrum-shattering polyrhythms. A synth that sounds like a harpsichord duetting with a buzz saw lets out a sustained, unbroken tone, the bass breaks into a sprint lock-step with the wailing guitar, and the drummer starts pummeling the kick and the toms in a primordially elegant weave.

"This band is fucking incredible," I yell.

"Look, no judgment, man," he yells through the music. "Personally? I think it's a little carceral to draw a line, any line, between one thing and another, in any situation."

EYES FOR GOVERNOR, painted across the fence of a house in southern Missouri, next to a Confederate flag and a MAGA sign.

No one gets to stay in the motel they want, but everyone gets to stay in the motel they deserve. Halfway across the country, both of us are irritable. Ruth has been vomiting every day and blames my driving. My car is making a disturbing, high-pitched grinding noise that I don't want to deal with because I am already hemorrhaging money on this trip. No one is allowed to talk about any of it.

"Have you heard anything about your interview from last month?" Ruth says, exiting a gas station bathroom, looking pale.

"Nope, not a word. Do you want to maybe go to a pharmacy?"

"Do you want to maybe take this car to a mechanic?"

"That sound is normal for Subarus. The engines idle rough. I think I understand my own car."

"I think I understand my own body."

We drive on in silence.

The best medicine, as they say, is advice.

Parable of Crystal Bridges

Walking past one of John Cage's Plexigrams—a boxlike object made up of rearrangeable plexiglass panels that allow the viewer to make a random arrangement of words and images, a classic Cagean chance operation—through the oculus of this art museum financed by family wealth wrung from business practices that have crippled people on a planetary scale for at least three successive generations, I approach a stunning, hypnotic Joan Mitchell painting. I gaze into its gauzy yellow shadows, the cooler tones of which seem to be trellising into my skeleton like a system of flowering vines. I recall a phrase Will sometimes uses when he encounters a little piece of the sublime: "I don't know whether to shit or go blind." While I stand there, the elderly patron next to me does in fact noisily shit his pants.

The sound is so incongruous with the setting that for a moment I think I've imagined it—but when the smell hits me, I turn from the painting and feel the blood drain from my face. Suddenly I lose vision in my left eye so forcefully that I have to sit down. I take a few deep breaths, trying not to panic. As the museum guests walk around me, a tide of color laps back up—but far too slowly.

If you need to "digest" art, it follows that you can choke on scenery; if chance requires an "operation," it isn't chance.

Parable of Joan Mitchell

Blue cage, teal cage, green cage, ochre cage, aqua cage, yellow cage, mustard cage, burgundy cage, red cage, rose cage, magenta cage, platinum cage, charcoal cage, chartreuse cage, puce cage, pink cage, lilac cage, sunset cage, sail cage, soil cage, salmon cage, knotted cage, clot cage, burnt sienna cage, rust cage, custard cage, snail shell cage, drip cage, grass cage, rhyme cage, diagonal cage, worm cage, circle cage, dot cage, clear cage, chrome cage, mail cage, air cage.

The Ozarks: rolling mountains and jagged cliffs cloaked with veils of falling water and vines, bombed by howling predators and rapid-fire chirping. A de-peopled, densely forested landscape. It's like nothing I've ever seen before. For the first time since Baltimore, I notice that I feel happy. A bird hidden in the darkening pine cries out, "Pizza! Lavender, lavender pizza!"

"I hate birds," Ruth sighs, gazing into the trees by our campfire.

"You don't hate birds," I instruct.

"I do. I'm not interested in them."

"You're a poet. What do you like if you hate birds?"

Ruth considers this for a moment. The logs crackle. Insects drone around us.

"I'm interested in trends."

"If you think about it, birds are evolution's trend."

"I'm getting in the tent and going to sleep."

Interested in trends. Interested? No, we love them. Each, in every patch of lichen that grows in the manifold crevices of the world's exquisite masonry, every speckled egg in every nest, for all the eons that they stand.

In the morning, after Ruth vomits, we hike out to a locally famous cave, a cave with a skylight where water ceaselessly pours, called Glory Hole Falls—the actual name of the waterfall, named after the glory of God. Light decants through the trickling stream, filling the cave with a soft glow. My knee hurts, but it's so beautiful that I barely notice. I turn to Ruth. She is crying, quietly.

"What's wrong?" I say.

"Just"—she wipes her face with her sleeve and points at the falling water—"look at all that information."

Parable of the Good Knee

His bad knee felt bad all the time. But his good knee felt like no knee at all.

Gasoline, I think to myself while filling the tank on the way out of Arkansas: the final land art.

We blow past the town of Dead Woman, Oklahoma. "What do you think the town is named for?" I say.

"Good question," Ruth says. "I'll look it up." She looks at her phone. "You're never going to believe this, but apparently a woman died in this town."

"Of natural causes?"

"She was murdered. It says the case is still unsolved." She stares out the window. We ride on in silence for a while.

"Listen, I'm sorry for the way I've been acting," she says, finally. "I know you're going through a tough time. I want to be a good friend to you. I'm just scared. I might have missed a day or two of birth control with Chester."

"I'm sorry I said we should go to a pharmacy a few days ago. It was none of my business."

"Let's find one in Amarillo," she says. A sustained screech issues from under the hood and a faint metallic smell wafts through the vents. "For real, are you not worried about your car?"

"I told you, Subaru engines idle rough. That sound is normal."

In the distance, a thin tongue of lightning flicks out of a thunderhead over a gargantuan cross rising out of the landscape, rain bearing down on the warm chrysalis of our mood. Then, fifty miles east of Amarillo, just outside Groom—the actual name of the town, named after a rancher named B. B. Groom, but more well-known, Ruth is in the middle of telling me, for its two-hundred-foot-tall cross—my car makes a terrible rattle, then stops right as a curtain of heavy rain sweeps over us.

In a rain of nearly biblical wetness, the roadside mechanic tells me my engine smells like metal on metal.

"What does that mean?" I say, soaking wet.

"When was the last time you got the oil changed?" he says in an enormous orange raincoat.

I don't have much to say to that. In the days before we left I'd been planning our two poetry readings extensively—composing three entire emails, sending two of them. Getting the oil changed before driving three thousand miles had not crossed my mind. Ruth, her hair matted to her face, looks at the ground and shakes her head.

The tow operator kindly drops Ruth off at Husband International Airport—the actual name of the airport, named after Amarillo native and astronaut Rick Husband, who died in the Space Shuttle Columbia disaster.

"They should just call it Dead Man Airport," she says. "Dead *Spaceman* Airport."

"Thanks for driving halfway across the country with me. Sorry I killed our car."

"Your car," she corrects. "All is forgiven. I'm sorry I'm not riding this out with you in Amarillo. I might need to see a doctor."

"Don't worry about me. Call after you pee on the stick. Love you."

"Call when you know what day you'll be in LA. Please be safe."

We hug it out in front of Departures. Then I get back in the tow truck and go straight to Brown Subaru—named after, I learn, the color of all food in Amarillo. I'm told the parts for the destroyed engine will arrive in ten days. It will run me close to five thousand dollars.

Rich with honor but devoid of sense. Rich with sense but devoid of shame. Rich with shame but devoid of worms.

No. Rich with shame *and* devoid of worms. And until the worms take this Husband of fate? His name is Richard. But his friends call him Rick.

Amarillo is beset by a heat wave that is surely the sign of someone, something trying to scour us from the earth. I stay in the cheapest, scariest motel in town, coincidentally or not within walking distance from Brown Subaru. I check my savings on my phone. After the engine is repaired, about twenty-five hundred dollars will remain. I sit on the edge of a very squeaky bed in a cube of arctic air-conditioning and try not to move. If I trip and break a bone and someone calls an ambulance for me, I'm fucked.

Without Ruth around, time feels strange—the hours don't so much pass as erase themselves from the clock. A state of nonexistence, like death—a going down for the big dirt nap.

"Howdy, boys—where y'all headed?"

"I'm fixin' to fix this engine, then I'm going down for my dirt nap."

Following a laser point across the floor or wall of a motel room is obviously only for cats or morons. But I think we can agree that following it through a lush forest or a chirping prairie at sunset sounds, quite frankly, very exciting.

Ruth texts me a photo of a pregnancy test: ||

"What are you going to do?" I ask her on the phone.

"I don't know. I'm trying to find the answer in myself."

"Have you told Chester?"

"Not yet. I've only told you—and Homer. Lucy and I will talk later today. Will and I have a phone date tomorrow. They're both worried, you know. I told them you're resourceful, even if you're an idiot."

"Thanks for fielding the inquiries." Will has texted me. Lucy has not.

"I don't know what to do," she sighs. "I never thought I'd be in this situation."

"We're Jews, Ruth. We don't sweat this. My great-grandmother would have objected more to getting a tooth pulled on a Saturday than getting an abortion on a Sunday. Walk right past those evil incels holding signs outside the clinic, look them dead in their black little eyes, and say, 'Shabbat Shalom, motherfuckers—'"

"It's not that at all," she snaps. "It's about what I want my life to look like."

We are both quiet.

"I always thought when I arrived at moments like this, it would be obvious," she continues. "Like life would make the decision for me. But it's not like that—if you're lucky, nothing is. For me, there is no good or bad decision—not until I've already made the choice and seen it play out. Terrifying. To find out which one is right I have to choose."

Parable of a Budding Grove

I sit reading *Within a Budding Grove*, the second book in Proust's *Search*, at the dealership, where the coffee is bad but free. For hours every day I read a few pages, pace to the garage, look for a sign of my car, and read a few more pages. No one speaks to me. A few days in, a mechanic approaches and asks where I'm from. When I tell him I'm from New York, he says that there are nice people everywhere, and that he understands, for example, that it is nicer in New York now than it was in the eighties, "with all the crime."

A different mechanic approaches a few mornings later and tells me that the parts have finally arrived. My car will be ready in a few hours. He is cautiously optimistic about how things are going, his words like a cool sea breeze. I thank him profusely. An hour or two passes. I open *Within a Budding Grove* to its last pages.

The final sentence reads, "And when Francoise removed the pins from the top of the window-frame, took down the cloths, and drew back the curtains, the summer day which she disclosed seemed dead, as immemorial, as a sumptuous millenary mummy from which our old servant had done no more than cautiously unwind the linen wrappings before displaying it, embalmed in its vesture of gold."

I read these words, and a soft electricity enters the top of my spine and exits through my limbs. As I look up from the page, the second mechanic looms over me. He says that my Forester's dead engine has been replaced, and that they've included a new timing belt free of charge.

I fly through the Texas Panhandle, New Mexico, and Arizona at ninety miles per hour. I have never felt so exhilarated or alone, an electric-blue dome vaulted over a seemingly infinite red vacancy.

In western Arizona, after what feels like days, the sun finally goes down. California within spitting distance, nearly at the border, I am so exhausted I can barely see. I get off the interstate, make three turns onto an abandoned dirt road, and pull over. I can rest my eyes here for an hour or two, wake before dawn, be on my way. I unroll my sleeping bag under a dense net of stars and lie flat on my back in a field next to the car, the universe reduced to three properties: darkness, light, and time. A coyote laughs in the distance. Seven years is nothing here. It oozes out of me and spills into this, a place that can take it.

I wake to a man standing over me holding a rifle. I seem to have overslept. The sun is blazing above the horizon. It must be almost a hundred degrees outside my sleeping bag; inside it is infernal, drenched with sweat.

"I don't know about New York, but Arizona is a stand-your-ground state, and this is my land. What's in the car? What's your line of work?"

The most important question of my life. I answer immediately, without thinking.

"Most of it," I sputter, "doesn't rhyme."

Horrified as I am to realize that my mouth is saying this, it's worse to know what's coming next.

"But recently a lot of it does."

"Excuse me? I don't know what the fuck you're on, but pack your shit and get off my property."

Eagerly, I do. As the Subaru kicks up dust, aimed at California, I check my phone. Just after nine. I have a voicemail from a New York number, from an hour ago.

"Good morning, D__," says a crisp voice. "I'm calling about your interview. We were impressed and very much enjoyed talking to you. We would like to offer you the position, with a starting date of Wednesday, the first of August. Please call us back."

I check my phone. Friday, July 27.

I call the super of the apartment without living cockroaches and tell him I can drop off the deposit in person at the beginning of the month.

I call Ruth to tell her I'm headed back to New York.

I turn the car around.

Being struck on the skull, second after second, with the blunt instrument of time.

Vertical clouds over the interstate, moving slowly, catching light like bits of a sail.

Locked outside the hour, sunlight left its boot print on his glad face.

Every light-year of their surfaces inked with nothing, save for a toss of fiery points: the scorpion, the swan, and the great bear drifting in their circuits, dropping silent gossip down upon his skin.

AUGUST

First day at the new job. My Senior Content Adjuster shows me around. I smile, try to seem competent, firmly pump hands, pray that sweat stains aren't showing through my new shirt, and am left to my work.

Instead of an open office plan, the new office has old-fashioned cubicles. The man in the cubicle directly to my left picks up the office landline and dials four numbers. The phone directly to the right of me rings.

"Hello?" says the colleague to the right.

"Hey," says the colleague to the left. "Do you have any gum?"

Imagine if, over dozens of eons, the percussively clicking song of the cicadas formed a full sentence, a question recorded on a trans-historical audio file; and when sped up to last only five seconds, the totality of their song—recorded over a span of time in which empires had risen and fallen, great symphonies had been written, celebrated, and forgotten, and death and laughter had abounded in equal measure—consists only of this inquiry:

D O Y O U H A V E A N Y G U M ?

In *The Guermantes Way*, our narrator, Marcel, tells us that his grandmother's true self appears, for the first time, over the telephone—true because she is there, by dint of being *only a voice*, without the armor of manners.

If the telephone reduced us to an essential quality of voice, email made us extra.

DO NOT PUT ANYTHING EXTRA IN THIS TOILET reads the sign in the office bathroom.

Fox News is on mute as I get my hair cut. Closed captioning reveals that the president is raving about why journalists are the enemy of the people, but I am more interested in the texture of his skin, a crinkled veil of damp ectoplasm that has quickly become as familiar to my nervous system as the moldy shower curtain I remember from my grandfather's bathroom. It contrasts strikingly with the buffed alabaster surface of his son-in-law, standing next to him. An elongated love child of a ventriloquist dummy and a night crawler, the son-in-law's silence is his greatest performance, almost a part of his body, his most powerful muscle, a force that seems to travel backward through time and space the longer you look into his glassy eyes. I wonder if he himself has reached through the screen to mute the TV in the barbershop. A Proustian character.

"Saddened by the misfortune of the Jews, remembering his friendship with Christians, increasingly mannered and affected as time went on for reasons to be revealed in due course, he now looked like a Pre-Raphaelite worm onto which hairs had been indecently grafted, like threads in the depth of an opal." (Proust, *The Guermantes Way*)

The barber wipes the last of the foam from his razor, slaps the back of my neck, and says, "Now you go back to school."

I finish loading boxes of books and thirdhand furniture into the apartment, swept clean of roach carcasses. The heat is nearly unbearable.

I unroll the rug and find two long cat whiskers. I place them in a small jar. Then I set up my new bed, turn on the fan, close my eyes, and sleep more deeply than I have in months.

The next morning I ride out to Coney Island alone. Two boys are horsing around on the boardwalk, about twelve years old, swiping a Juul back and forth from each other's pockets, passing a skateboard under their feet, cutoff shirts and ripped jeans, punching each other, laughing, kissing with yarmulkes between their lips as a kind of wall. Mountainous, creamy clouds float above the sand behind the Wonder Wheel. A dragnet of black-headed gulls swarm a palm print umbrella, frozen in the air. I haven't been here since Ruth and I began our road trip. Some summer this has been.

"How are you feeling?" I ask her on the phone.

"Bad," she says. "I'm still nauseous all the time."

"Have you decided what you're going to do?"

"Well—it's kind of crazy. I had an appointment at the clinic the other day. I told Chester I would go alone. It was something I had to face myself. I expected cross-toting pigs to be yelling at women outside, and they were. But when I got there—Chester had brought a whole setup of amps and looping pedals hooked up to his car battery. He was blasting drone clarinet over them. They were inaudible."

"Jesus," I say.

"I know—enraging! He defied me." She is quiet for a moment. "But also—there was something romantic about it. When I got to the waiting room, I just didn't want to go through with it."

I'm speechless.

"I tossed almost an entire bottle of kombucha on those fuckers outside as I was leaving. Couldn't let Chester outdo me. Anyway, we're looking at an Aries due date—like you. So whoever this baby is they're going to love being the center of attention."

Morning astrology report on the subway: "Fuck a Libra, I'll punch a Libra motherfucker. Fuck a Leo, fuck a Virgo, and fuck Trump. But Obama was fucked-up too. Obama started a war too, if you know your history. Stop it with that face."

I stop by the old apartment to pick up a couple of things. Lucy opens the door and hugs me awkwardly. We haven't seen each other all summer. The place is the same, but all the photos of the two of us have been stashed away.

"How've you been?" I say.

"I'm okay." The cats purr and smash their faces into her ankles. They don't seem to remember me. "Did you hear Ruth's news?"

"I did. She told me the other day."

Silence.

"Anyway," I continue, "I should probably grab my stuff."

"I heard you got a job," Lucy says. "Congratulations. I'm proud of you. I hope you're happier there."

"Thanks for letting me come by. It's good to see you, Lucy."

"Wait!" she says, as I am about to leave. "You forgot your blazer." She gets it from the closet, drapes it over my shoulder, gives my arm a squeeze, and locks the door behind me.

"After escorting the Princess of Parma to her carriage, M. de Guermantes picked up my greatcoat with the words, 'Let me help you into your skin.'" (Proust, *The Guermantes Way*)

Dream, 8/17

"Here's the million-dollar question: are you ennobled, or merely accredited?"

Parable of Improvement

The arts and community center where I now work has not only a swimming pool but a concert hall. Passing by the concert hall, I catch a pianist performing a Beethoven sonata during sound check. I stop and, for several minutes, lose myself in the sad drift of the keys.

Above the pianist's head, beyond the ceiling richly decorated in late-nineteenth-century faux bois style, elderly New Yorkers swim their afternoon laps. I imagine the notes of the sonata vibrating up into the air, through the architecture and heavily chlorinated water, gently hammering into their skin as they splash up and down the lanes.

I decide to sign up for the free gym membership offered as a perk at the job. My Senior Content Adjuster smiles as she signs the form.

"If working here doesn't improve your quality of life, then something is wrong," she says. "I'm glad you're taking advantage of this. Enjoy."

I had not thought it possible that a job could improve one's life. I had always assumed labor to be wholly out of sync with pleasure, something we did for the paycheck, to stave off death.

Later, as I change in the gently mildewed locker room, from two floors below, through the ventilation ducts, very faintly, I hear a crowd erupt into applause. Two octogenarian men walk past me, still wet from the pool and nude except for towels draped around their shoulders.

"Those old Broadway musicals are fabulous," one of them says, his voice like two cascades of sand sifting into one another midair, "stuff like *Guys and Dolls* and *Smokey Joe's Café*. But some of these new musicals just make you want to kill yourself."

The other turns to me as they walk by and, seeing my hasty attempt to cover myself with a towel, theatrically rolls his eyes.

He turns back to his friend. "At our age you can't waste your time on new musicals."

Today, my alma mater's literary journal publishes a poem of mine called "Dumpster," and I am invited to come to campus to give a reading in October.

When it rains, it dumps.

Dream, 8/29

Smoke pouring out of my open laptop, the screen's magnesium white glow all but obscured. When I wake, the sun is blazing red just above the horizon, its hot reflection slicing off the water.

I blink. The ocean blinks back.

FALL NOTEBOOK, 2018

SEPTEMBER

At my old job, I wrote descriptions of objects. At my new job, I write descriptions of talks, concerts, Jewish life classes and holiday services, and other events.

Once I was in the business of selling objects. Now I am in the business of selling time.

But how am I to use the time I don't sell?

I search through my notebooks.

My mom texts me to remind me to wish my great-uncle Isidore a happy birthday. He has just turned one hundred.

Parable of Uncle Isidore

Sep 2, 2018, 1:13 PM

Dear Uncle Isidore,

Just wanted to drop you a quick note to wish you a very happy birthday—100 is a big one! I hope this finds you well and that we can see each other again soon.

Lots of love,
D__

Sep 3, 2018, 1:26 PM

Dear D__: Thank you for the greeting. I just read your "Dumpster" poem. Congratulations. I will be learning how to interpret your style of poetry. Across the street from where I live, there was recently a dumpster, into which all the furniture, house cleaning equipments, lamps, tools, books, were being tossed. I knew those neighbors well. Although the debris never existed in close association before, it now did. Examined closely, as by an anthropologist, they revealed an entire type of life.

For some reason, I was always interested in poetry. In fact, the only book I ever kept after graduating from high school was "The Golden Treasury," a book of old English poetry. So, it was only a matter of time before one of my parents' greatgrand whatevers would be a poet. Excelsior!

Love, Isidore

Sep 4, 2018, 11:31 AM

Dear Isidore,

Thank you so much for this note. I'm delighted that you read the poem. I've wondered if there's a recessive poetry gene in our family—I remember seeing you reading Keats at Grandpa's memorial, a favorite of mine as well.

On a related note—I wanted to run something by you. Lately I've been keeping a scrapbook of sorts, very different from Keats, or "Dumpster," or really anything else I've written, which includes (among other things) pieces of overheard dialogue and lots of found language that I myself did not write. I wonder how you'd feel about me including some portion or all of your previous email in the scrapbook. It's an experiment, so it might never come to anything, or it's possible that someday down the road I would put it in a book—too early to tell. If this is confusing or you'd prefer I not include it, it's completely fine—just say so and I'll leave it out. Let me know what you think.

Love,
D__

Sep 5, 2018, 12:07 PM

Dear D__: You can quote me if you wish. I just read a poem by Wisława Szymborska entitled "The Stagecoach." In a sense, a stagecoach is a dumpster of people, and she gets inspiration from it.

Love, Isidore

At the beach on Labor Day, Will and I—sunburned and basic—suffer the music of the proximate tweens with quiet dignity, stoned out of our gourds. A couple of extraordinarily ripped men walk by. "Do you think my pecs should be more chiseled?" I say.

"They don't have to be, man. You already have a chiseled chest—of song."

The screaming child beside us has reached a pitch of exaltedness such that no amount of sherbet can calm him down.

"Do you think you'll ever be a dad?" Will says.

"I can't imagine not being able to drop everything and go to the beach on Labor Day. You know? My time—I value it. But I'm happy for Ruth. She'll be a great mom."

"Totally. Here's to Ruth." We tap our Narragansetts together.

"Did you and Ruth ever talk about kids when you were together?" I say.

"I wanted to, but she said she couldn't see it with me."

"Damn. I didn't know that."

"She said I refused to grow up."

We each sit with that for a moment, not speaking—the wheels turning slowly, the scales trembling behind our eyes, a cloaked phantom of steely-eyed reason silently tangoing with the vaporous purple clown that has taken up residence in our brains.

"Do you think you'll start dating again soon?" he finally says, eager to move on.

A man on the towel next to us, also apparently unencumbered by family or partnership, is reading a self-help book entitled *Deep Work*. He too is vaping heavily, clouds bearing the smell of synthetic waffles and syrup billowing out of his nostrils, like a dragon.

"I don't think I'm ready yet," I say.

"Entire birds, consisting of a black dot and two lines," Will says after a while, squinting out over the horizon. "Can you imagine?"

"I'm taking one more dunk before we leave," I say.

I run down to the water and dive into the waves. I swim out just beyond the body surfers, and am about to swim back—but there in the water, treading water a few feet away, is Fatima, the colleague from the job I lost last year.

I look at her, not quite knowing whether to say hello. She catches me staring and glares back, not recognizing me at first. Then she shakes her head and her face breaks into a professional smile.

"Oh my God, hi!" she says, swimming over to me, tilting her head up to keep it above the water. "How are you?"

It is a slight shock to see her—less because of the coincidence of running into one another than the fact of seeing a former colleague in the ocean. Here we are, bobbing in the surf, with wet hair. As coworkers, we saw one another every day, an acute intimacy—but swimming in the same body of water is not something that ever crossed my mind until this moment. But I suppose I should get used to the idea, considering my new workplace has a pool.

She gives me the gossip from the old company. After the mass exodus, she has continued as a "transitional copywriter"—a customer service and shipping agent. I ask how our former boss is doing.

"It's crazy, actually—I don't know," she says, shading her eyes from the sun. "About six weeks ago he stopped responding to my emails. Just ghosted! I called the parent company, and apparently he no longer works there. I'm the only one left." She pauses. "I did finally get that cool gray couch I had been wanting."

"Damn," I say. "Well—congrats! Nice to see you. We should get a drink and catch up for real."

"Totally," she says.

The waves lap at our shoulders. We both know that we have no reason to meet again.

I swim back to shore.

At the office, as I continue to be ravaged by the hammer that is a series of years on Earth, I am surprised to find that I have more occasion to use the word "than" than "then"—that we may never discover how many *r*'s there really are in the word "appearing."

I am tasked with writing a description for a series of Jewish youth groups—partially secular, partially observant, the kind of group my friends and I used to attend at our temple on Monday nights when we were kids, bribed by our parents and the rabbis with a steady flow of free pizza. It's never been my thing. But nothing is my thing.

I close my eyes and try imagining what my parents would have wanted to hear to sign me up for something like this. Then I try to imagine what I would want to hear. I write:

> How do you *be* a Jewish child in 2018?

Nice, I think to myself. Still got it. I email it off to my Senior Content Adjuster.

She stops by my desk. "Thank you for that description," she says. "I've made a few adjustments. I wonder if perhaps you should attend some of our Jewish life events, to get a feel for things here."

Parable of the Rebrand

I am in a meeting with the director of our performance programming. For decades, she has curated an impressive commedia dell'arte series on Wednesdays called Mimes in the Afternoon. The series was surprisingly popular for years. But in the last decade, the target demographic—both audience and donors—has begun to expire.

Mimes in the Afternoon is being rebranded for a younger crowd. It will be rescheduled for Friday nights, to appeal to those who cannot take time off work in the middle of the week to see a prestige mime performance, though no one admits out loud that this is still a futile proposition—not many young adults interested in the latest innovations in silent clown technology will come to Midtown on a Friday night after work, because for three decades real estate prices have pushed them far away from institutions like ours, into smaller and smaller apartments in the outer boroughs, with salaries that have stayed more or less the same. This means that the rebrand needs to *pretend* to appeal to millennials—to satisfy institutional anxiety about our cultural relevance—while dog-whistling to boomers to make them feel both hip and nostalgic, and buy tickets. This delicate conundrum is what copywriters are made for.

"Mimes in the Afternoon is an iconic part of this institution," says the indignant programmer. "It was always on Wednesday. Always in the afternoon. It worked. Why does it need to change?"

"Well, it's always good to try a fresh perspective," I say.

"How long have you been here, five minutes?" she says. "Try me in five years with a fresh perspective. Sorry, I'm agitated. It's not your fault."

"No worries. I've got a few ideas. What if we call the series You've Got Mimes?"

"Not bad. Not bad at all. But it doesn't convey the fact that it's now on Fridays. What do you think of calling it . . ." She snaps her fingers. "I've got it. Friday Night Lights!"

"I think that one's taken. It's a show about a high school football team in Texas."

"Oh," she says. "Well, I have been looking for something new to watch."

"Let's stick with the Friday theme. What about . . . When Miming Met Friday?"

"That one's a little clunky."

"That's fair," I say, getting nervous—I don't know many more Meg Ryan movies to riff on.

"The name has to convey *exactly* what the series is, as clearly as possible. Clarity is the most important thing. People should know that it's new, but also exactly the same. Wait a minute. I've got it." She rubs her temples. "I see it. We'll call it"—she spreads her arms out above her—"Mimes in the Afternoon on Friday Night."

"I'm not sure—"

"Mimes in the Afternoon on Friday Night. That's exactly what it is. It's perfect. Thank you. The suits are going to love it. You were right—it *is* important to get a fresh perspective."

It's been fifteen years since I've gone to temple. I expect the Yom Kippur service to differ from the services I remember from childhood. But it is essentially the same. Meditative. Somber. Maudlin. Moving. Boring. Interesting. Boring again. Intensely boring.

The crowd issues impressed murmurs when the shofar is blown with great force. Everything is as it was, down to the mirrored surface of that cantor's bald head as he sings the Kaddish.

Cast your pocket lint into this river.

Give your lint to this intern.

Parable of a Bell

I am ringing a call bell at a bar, a bell I dug out of the bottom of one of my boxes. Will is with me, and Lucy, who is here to faithfully follow an unwritten law: when we need advice about anything related to poetry, we show up, no matter what. I am trying to convince them that using this bell in the reading of my notebooks at my alma mater, to signify the breaks, is a good idea. It sounds sharp and clear, lovely really, if a little loud.

"Don't you think it's a little—theatrical?" Will says.

"What if you were to just, like, knock on the lectern," Lucy suggests, knocking the table twice. "That could be a good solution."

"I like the way the bell sounds," I say, stubbornly ringing it for emphasis.

"Lucy's right," Will says, the traitor. "I like the knocking idea. It sounds like fate at the door."

"The bell makes it sound like you're asking for service," Lucy says. "Do you want that?"

"Maybe I do," I shoot back, dinging for emphasis, digging my heels in, rapidly regressing.

"Listen. The bell is stupid," Lucy says, losing her patience. "It's the sonic equivalent of wearing a fedora. Grow up. You can't use props at poetry readings. We're trying to prevent you from embarrassing yourself."

"That's not your problem anymore," I snap, slamming my hand down on the bell. A woman at the bar does not turn to us but speaks so I can hear.

"Every time that bell rings an angel loses its fucking wings."

In the end I decide to knock.

"Did your weekend have a highlight?" says my colleague on the left, on the phone with my colleague to the right. The office lights flicker. Coffee is steaming from each of their mugs. My colleague to the right thinks for a moment, twisting the phone cord around her finger.

"The highlight of my weekend was time," she says.

OCTOBER

A folk song about counting.

A folk song about imitating a police siren.

A folk song containing the lyric "I only love my bed and my mama, I'm sorry."

A folk song containing the lyric "The only tune that the fiddle would play was 'O, the Wind and the Rain.'"

Parable of Bloodlines

I travel to rural Ohio to give a poetry reading at my alma mater. I do not bring the bell. The reading is well received.

"How do you write poetry that's true but that also isn't overly personal?" a student asks me afterward. I don't know how to respond.

Later, I eat dinner with Ron, a beloved former religious studies professor. Ron is one of the gentlest men I've ever known, possessed of a gentleness verging on genius: inquisitive but never hectoring, polite but genuinely so—there exists a spiteful politeness in the Midwest—thoughtful but silly, grave but cheerful, meandering but focused. In the class I took with him in college, called "Meanings of Death," a survey of death and mourning rituals across world religions, one of the assignments was to write a eulogy for someone who was still alive. To this day there is a bit of this assignment in every poem I write.

Ron is now retired. He has many close friends in town, but he has never married or had children. At dinner he gleefully describes his retirement plans—writing a murder mystery set in a seminary, a story based on events he witnessed as a young man.

Our dinner ends and we say our goodbyes, wish each other well. The night is open before me in my old stomping grounds where I too might be inspired to write a murder mystery, if I could only witness one. But I am too old to hang out with the students and too young to pass the evening with the professors, who all go to bed early anyway. A beautiful fall night, the rest of which passes without incident. I sleep poorly.

I wake before dawn to catch a shuttle back to the airport in Columbus. A man about Ron's age pulls up in a sedan in the dark and introduces himself as Don.

I dislike Don immediately. He chats with me in the car like a genial prison guard. Conversation in this context is a kind of disinfectant spray against intimacy—or, if you'd like, pure form. He is unwilling to hazard the exquisite awkwardness of sitting with a stranger in silence, which I cherish, but also seems unwilling to talk about anything that actually matters to either of us.

He asks me what I "do," and when I tell him I'm a poet, he asks what sports I like. I ask him what he "does"—he tells me he is a retired math teacher. He used to teach at the local high school, a place "with a good reputation." I am already exhausted, counting the seconds until I can get out of the car. The cornfields roll out in the darkness like an infinite bruise.

"What do your parents think of the fact that you're a poet?" he says suddenly.

I am taken aback. Not because the question is rude, but I am surprised he wants to go there. I explain that they don't always *get* my poems, per se—but they respect my choice to let life revolve around poetry even when it perplexes them.

"As long as you can pay the bills, I guess," Don says. I don't mention the fact that until recently I was unemployed for eight months.

"Do you have kids?" I say. There is a heavy pause, and I realize that this is the question he has been fishing for all along. And yet he seems reluctant to answer.

"Two daughters. About your age."

"What do they do?"

"The older one worked at a blood bank outside of Erie for seven years, but she got divorced and had to come home. She's thirty-five. Still *looking for a man*." He emphasizes this last phrase as if he can't quite fathom it, a piece of slang that is beyond him.

"I see. Nice that you get to see her more often."

"Yeah, she's around."

"And what about the younger one?"

A heavy pause. "She works at the Rite Aid."

"Does she like it?"

"They're good to her. She has problems. Developmental disabilities. They work with her."

"Oh, well that's great. Good to have a job." I am really starting to hate myself.

"She hangs out with a lot of lowlifes."

"What do you mean?"

"People see that she's slow and take advantage of her."

"That's—just horrible. I'm so sorry." I don't know what to say.

"It's very painful."

I can't speak for a moment. "Are she and her sister close?"

"Yeah, they're close."

"That's good," I say automatically. "It's good they have one another."

"Yeah. Well—no. That's not actually true. They fight a lot."

"Oh, all siblings fight."

"Well, the way they fight—they shouldn't be fighting like that anymore. They're adults."

"I see."

The sun still isn't up, but the corn is glowing a little now, a pale wave of husks rolling out before us.

"It's getting to the point where my wife and I are starting to wonder what we did wrong."

We both stare dead ahead at the road, suddenly united in silence.

"Do you imagine you'll ever become a father?" he says after a while.

"I had, uh—cats at one point," I say directly into the windshield. "I'm not sure about children."

"Not the same," he says, shaking his head. "Not even close." He takes a deep breath. He turns the sports report on.

"Do you think the Cavs can win without LeBron?" I ask, flooded with relief, though I realize that to Don this question is the equivalent of "What kind of poetry do you write?"

"No." He laughs. "No, I don't think so." He changes the station.

The news. The president has said something, somewhere, and someone is talking about it.

We are halfway to the airport. The clouds are turning pink.

"I hate politics," he says, smiling.

In the airport, staring out over the tarmac, I think: people are like bricks. Sometimes you're the brick that gets thrown through a window, and sometimes you're the brick in a private huddle with its wall.

"People in society are too apt to think of a book as a sort of cube one side of which has been removed so the author can 'put in' the people he meets." (Proust, *Sodom and Gomorrah*)

As a person in society, I've smoked just enough weed to be seriously troubled by this cube theory of literature. What happens to the people the author puts in the cube? What if the author climbs in with them? What goes on once the cube is closed?

Weep in relation to x.

Weep for x.

X is weeping.

Dream, 10/24

I am sitting down for a meal in a dark, candlelit dining room. Gathered around the table is my family. Some of them are very old and wearing shawls. My great-grandmothers. They are talking privately to one another.

This dream feels different from others—like a message. Then a gunman walks into a synagogue in Pittsburgh and murders eleven people.

Names: they're not photography. They don't look like you.

Names: they're not photography. They do, nevertheless, depict you.

Parable of Glass

At the office, we are shaken. At a prominent Jewish institution, it is not difficult to imagine that we could be the next target.

An American flag has been hung in the lobby near the extra security. I find this confusing—the shooter, a white nationalist, was apparently motivated by a conspiracy theory that white Christian Americans are being "replaced" by Jews. Hanging an American flag in a Jewish institution's lobby feels off today—like putting a cross up in the waiting room of Planned Parenthood after an abortion clinic is bombed, or making students in Gaza recite US tax code after Israel launches a missile at their school. In our lobby, in fact—by the logic of some silent rhyme—an Israeli flag has been hung next to the American one.

I am waiting in a conference room for the resident rabbi. The meeting was scheduled before the attack—today, it is going to hit different. As he enters the room, I stand to greet him. He regards me gravely and signals to sit with a wave of his hand.

"No need to stand on ceremony," he says, a falsehood so antiquated that it needs its own genre, a closer cousin to myth than lie. I know someone with an executive mindset when I meet them—this guy wants me to rise to shake his hand. And he doesn't want to seem like he wants that. He is young, almost exactly my age, but something in his voice—rich, sonorous, touched by ancient nicotine—lends him a certain gravity. "Please, sit down," he says.

"How are you?" I say.

"It's a difficult day. But not a surprising one. There's nothing in the world that's older than the hatred of Jews."

"I always knew that T. rex at the Natural History Museum was an antisemite." The words almost spasm out of me. I am met with stony silence.

"Sorry," I say, "that was inappropriate. Unprofessional. I use humor as a coping mechanism."

"Listen, D__. This is a moment when we need to be absolutely united."

Sympathetic as I am to unity as a general idea, who he means by "we" is unclear. Jewish people? He and I? The ecosystem of our office, where I serve as an entry-level employee and he has landed in the C-suite in his early thirties? I feel as if I have wandered into a kind of spiritual locker room where the mirrors are all fogged up.

"So don't worry about it," he says.

I exhale. "What can I do for you?"

"Next month, as I'm sure you know, is the eightieth anniversary of the November Pogrom, or Kristallnacht."

"Yes," I say. "Yes. I definitely do know that."

"We need to come up with a good name for the memorial program. It's going to be a somber evening. But also a joyous one, because here, we are all survivors. Clarity is the most important thing. People should know exactly what they're going to get. But you're the writer—*you* tell *me*. I'd like to run something by you. What do you think about"—he spreads his arms out above him—"Kristallnacht 2018."

"Uh," I say.

"Kristallnacht 2018. It's simple. Clear. What do you think? It's good, isn't it?"

"It's up to you, of course. I'm just not sure Kristallnacht 2018 strikes quite the right tone."

"Interesting." He furrows his brow. "Why would you say that?"

"It sounds like a very scary version of Coachella."

"I see." He reflects on this. In a brisk, seamless motion—pure muscle memory, it seems—he fishes a Juul from his blazer and pulls on it, the small indicator light swelling to life. He stares out the window and releases a small plume of vapor from the side of his mouth. I say nothing. In an instant, his eyes flick back to me and go wide. He turns red. "Oh, whoops," he says, shoving the Juul in his pocket. "Sorry about that. I'm—trying to quit."

"Please, no worries at all," I say. "Like you said, this is a time when we need to be absolutely united."

"Anyway," he says, recovering. "What would you suggest instead, as a name for that program?"

I clasp my hands and look at the ceiling. "What about something like—oh, I don't know—Remembering the Night of the Broken Glass?"

He sits back in his chair and folds his hands under his chin. His gaze bores into me.

"That is direct. That is very good, D__. We can use that. Thank you."

Halloween in the backyard of a Brooklyn watering hole. The air is cool and crisp, the mood is festive, people are chatting over beers by a nice crackling fire, but I am drinking alone. The midterm election looms like a glittering pus-Christmas. Soon this bar will close for good and a putrid luxury high-rise will be erected where I sit. But none of that is what's gnawing at me.

No one is in a costume except for one woman dressed as Waldo, in a striped red and white sweater, glasses, and hat. Another is wearing a jack-o'-lantern sweatshirt, but this doesn't count.

Actually, it appears that Waldo's boyfriend is also dressed as Waldo.

But where am I?

When in Rome, burn.

NOVEMBER

It's been a while since a poem has come to me—have I written even one since Lucy and I broke up? This isn't necessarily a bad thing. You only write the poem when you're ready for it. But it's hard to deny that lately, within the general vicinity of my selfhood—a grid of neurons, gut bacteria, and THC molecules where electrical signals pulse at semiregular intervals to make me eat, sleep, worry, laugh, see my friends, and perhaps write a poem—something is rotten. I feel like a devolved spongelike object out of whom personality—not poetry—sometimes sloshes like a faintly sulfurous goo wiped up from under the sink of the universe, electrical signals hissing dangerously through it.

I keep thinking about what that student asked after the reading last month. How do you write poetry that's true but that also isn't overly personal? You have to maintain equilibrium in the grid of selfhood. If you don't, you're left with a stinking puddle of electric rot: pure personality.

The therapist's office is on the Upper East Side. A white noise machine hums in the corner. The décor is old-fashioned but fancy. The carpets thick. The overhead light fixtures decked out in crystal.

The wood of the furniture seems to contain more wood than my furniture at home. She opens the door to her office exactly on time and beckons me inside.

"Why don't you tell me why you're here," she says.

"I feel stuck."

She stares at me.

Suddenly obedient to anything I can construe as an order, I tell her everything: losing my old job, unemployment, Lucy and me, living with my parents in the suburbs, the road trip, having a rifle pulled on me in Arizona, the new job. At some point I realize I am hoarse from yelling.

"So that's why I'm here," I finish.

She nods. "Our time is almost up. For next week, I'd like you to try something. Go to the store and buy yourself a blank journal. In this journal, I'd like you to record everything, every detail that you remember, about when you masturbate."

"What?" I say.

"Every detail. Which hand do you use? What do you think about? What about the light?"

"What about the smell of the light?" I say, quoting Ashbery's "How Much Longer Will I Be Able to Inhabit the Divine Sepulcher," pleased with myself.

"What about the smell of the light?" she says, expressionless.

I feel that it would not be productive to explain the reference. "But, uh," I stammer, "what if I don't masturbate this week?"

She says nothing.

"Well, fine, but—I already keep this notebook." I pull it from my bag to show her. "Do I really have to get a new one? I think I forgot to mention—I'm actually a poet."

"A notebook is not a journal," she says. "And this is not poetry."

I feel a strange panic rising in my chest. "I don't think this is going to work," I say.

"Why is that?"

"You're not in my insurance network," I lie. There's no way this person understands me.

"Listen," she says, untroubled. "You? You can't go through life like this. You'll be back. I'm certain. Find some way to get the money if you must—perhaps you could ask your parents. In the meantime, I'd like to leave you with something important to consider."

I am irritated. "What is it?"

"It's very difficult to say what you feel."

I wait for her to continue, but she just stares at me.

"What I feel? Or what one feels, generally?"

She stares at me.

"That," I say, now quite angry, "is so fucking boring."

"Yes," she says calmly, without hesitation. "It is."

My mouth hangs open. My hands are tingling, ears ringing. I feel almost violently perceived, suddenly overwhelmed by real gratitude.

"Thank you," I say.

She nods.

"As when, in a stretch of country which one thinks one does not know and which in fact one has approached from a new direction, after turning a corner one finds oneself suddenly emerging on to a road every inch of which is familiar, but one had simply not been in the habit of approaching it that way, one suddenly says to oneself: 'Why, this is the lane that leads to the garden of my friends the X——s; I'm only two minutes from their house,' and there, indeed, is their daughter who has come out to greet one as one goes by . . ." (Proust, *The Captive*)

What is a day such that, passing through a handful of them, it can change the body irrevocably into what it almost is, but isn't?

WINTER NOTEBOOK, 2018/19

DECEMBER

"How are you feeling?" I ask Ruth on FaceTime.

"Good!" she says. "My feet are sore. Chester has been great. He's making dinner. Say hi."

She turns the phone to a tall, square-jawed man in an apron, standing in the kitchen and stirring a large pot. I haven't seen Chester in years, but he seems to have not aged at all.

"Hey, D__!" he says, waving a large spoon. I always liked him. I wave back.

"Look," Ruth says, turning the phone to her stomach. "She's kicking."

Through the screen, a shape flickers and slides under the surface of Ruth's stomach, like a creature in an ancient lake. I am genuinely shocked and moved.

"Holy shit," I say.

"Have you decided what you're going to do?" She turns the screen back to her face.

"About what?"

"Dating. Maybe it's time."

"Why do you say that?" I ask. This particular angle of forceful suggestion is out of character for her.

She hesitates and shrugs. "Just a thought. But I can help you set up a profile for an app if you want. Could be cute."

I consider this. "Sure, why not."

"Great. Actually, I already started one for you."

"You—what? You did?"

"Just a little PowerPoint deck for staging. I'll let you review the pictures I chose later. Now. The prompt is 'In my free time I like to . . .' What do you like to do when you get home from work?"

"Smoke weed and listen to Gregorian chant."

"We can workshop that. Let's move on to the next one. 'A shower thought I recently had . . .'"

"Can I get bubonic plague just on my penis?"

"You're not making this easy."

"Sorry, *may* I get bubonic plague just on my penis?"

"You're impossible."

"But it's true! I did think that in the shower the other day!"

I receive some photos of myself from Ruth.

He is splayed across the bed like a statuesque bag of fingerling potatoes.

His head is like a giant peanut with a face-shaped infection. And people tell him that this infection is handsome.

Fortune cookie: WHEN IN ANGER, SING THE ALPHABET.

Is it really so difficult to say what you feel? The whole point of having a way with words, I've always thought, is that words say it for you.

"For every person, even the humblest, has under his control those little familiar creatures, at once alive and reclining in a sort of torpor upon the paper: the characters of his handwriting which he alone possesses." (Proust, *The Fugitive*)

The alarm rings at seven thirty. Christmas morning. I turn it off, close my eyes, and see a black plane of dancing letters. I open my eyes and look at the clock again. It says 11:11.

Every alphabet, a standing order. Every second, a temporary conspiracy.

And just like that, for the first time in months, a poem comes to me.

Poem

A bell can do everything.
A bell can die entering
A bell called debt *exeunt* fate,
A bell cannibalizing dew's extinction feature, gladly
A bell, cancels description's error for good.
A bell's chorus doesn't extract feeling, giving heaven incineration's jejune kiss
A bell craves; daughters elemental, flinty gossip, hating instinctively
A bell's culmination; dangles effort's fleet gridlock here in
A bell's creaturely domain, echoing friendship's ghostly hate-integer
A bell calculates. Dirty errand, flat glamour
A bell cleans darkly, equivalent feature gilding
A bell crying distant emergency, for
A bell's cadaver debuts eating
A bell, clapping dim edges.

I wake and it's winter. Some note sounds off from the center of my corpus.

Ear against some other life, what is lost in translating penury to opulence?

The morning of New Year's Eve, on the train to work, someone yelling, "Everyone knows this FBI shit is dead—making your living off of making somebody else's life miserable is dead. It's over."

Do you hear what I hear?

Parable of Contact

My favorite holiday has always been New Year's Eve. The only holiday about which I feel truly religious, as it celebrates the only lineage everyone who has ever drifted through this place shares, from worm to worm: time.

Will and Lucy and I meet at a bar, where we play a mind-meld game. The rules: to start, two people say a random word at the same time. Then when two people think they have discovered the word that represents the exact midpoint between the original two words—the midpoint between "ocean" and "puddle" might be "lake," for example, or "water"—they say "contact," and try to say the midpoint word in unison.

"Clover," says Will. "Cheese," says Lucy.

"Contact!" I yell over the noise at the bar. "Contact," Will says.

At the same time, Will says "cow" and I say "graze."

"What's betwixt 'cow' and 'graze'?" Will says, drunk.

Lucy and I look at one another. “Contact,” we both say. Then, in unison, “Flies.” We high-five.

“Nice,” Will says. “Creepy but nice. Next round.”

“M. C. Escher,” Lucy says. “Chemtrails,” I say. Will suddenly looks electrified.

“Contact!” he bellows. “Rush Limbaugh’s nipples!”

Lucy, on the verge of wetting herself, runs to the bathroom. I’m laughing so hard I can barely breathe. “What’s so funny?” Will yells. “Why is that funny?”

Lucy returns a minute before midnight. “I’m glad we’re still friends,” I say.

“Me too.” She smiles. “Listen, I need to tell you though—I’ve started going on dates. I’m sorry to bring it up. I just don’t want you to find out from someone else.”

So this is why Ruth was so adamant about me getting on a dating app.

“Of course. I’m happy for you.” As I say it, I realize it’s true. “I’ll probably do the same soon.” Everyone at the bar starts counting down.

The clock strikes midnight, the ball drops, and the place erupts into “Auld Lang Syne.” Lucy throws her arm around my shoulder.

"Happy New Year," she says. "I'm glad we're still in each other's lives." She pauses. "And that our lives are changing."

Will, singing loud and off-key, grabs my face and plants a kiss on my forehead. I laugh and give him a smooch on the cheek. He shoots me a look of disgust. "That's it, you little pussy? You're not even going to give me some tongue?"

We sloppily make out. Around us, the bar cheers.

Near the end of Proust's *Search*, marveling at his long, winding sentences, I don't feel that I know him so much as that his words know one another, intimately, in a delicate social system—subject and object ambling along old garden pathways, through the streets, trading places in crowded parlors and empty bedrooms, tipping their hats and bowing to one another as they pass, strolling on, driven forward and away from one another by the gravitational force of time.

But every now and then, he delivers a quick gut punch.

"So what I believed to be nothing to me was simply my entire life." (Proust, *The Fugitive*)

Depends on your definition of "entire."

A faint but crystalline mumbling, like business dealings or distant television, fell ceaselessly from their lips.

JANUARY

Contrary to New Year's Eve, New Year's Day feels distinctly, uncannily, depressingly American. The only way to face it is to go to the movies.

North by Northwest

The line between poetry and cigarettes
Is like the line between frames in a film
Or the line between mouth and script
One always crossing the other

Line by line he makes his way
Blue lines, white lines, brown lines, gray
The line a costume cloaking his tongue
The line of that suit as it hangs off a man

A line of attack and a line of flight
By plane or train, wilderness lines
The velocity of escape you trace in a line
As a building lines the space it shades

An actor's body emitting lines
Washington's stone face glaring through pines
The line you smoke in lines of smoke
The line you strike on lines to light it

Winter deploys its smile out of order.

Winter translates its eyes into lines.

Parable of Courtly Love

"We have a few specials tonight," says our server. "For our vegetarians, I have a broccolini-wad tartine, tickled with pink Himalayan rainwater and butterfly-kissed with fermented dandelion hair aioli. That comes with a side of piping hot beans. For our meat-eaters"—he winks at me—"I have bongmilk-battered beef poppers, deep fried and smothered in a locally sourced bechamel–Four Loko sauce, served on a bed of wilted iceberg. Finally, I really recommend our self-harmed salmon. It's exquisite tonight. That's going to be mouth-slurped in an octopus headcheese and impaled with a micro–peanut butter and jelly sandwich flag flying half-mast on a caramelized pig finger."

"I'll have the plant wad," says my date.

"Excellent choice," the server says, turning to me. "And for the gentleman?"

I have never met up with someone via dating app before. My date's profile tells me that she just completed her final semester of coursework for a PhD in physics at Columbia, her most controversial opinion is that she drinks iced coffee all year long, she is not from the United States and would like her prospective suitors to guess what country she is from—my guess is Turkey, but I am not positive and am afraid to ask—and while she does not smoke cigarettes, she does occasionally smoke weed. Her name is listed as "P." She's smart, cute, and a little mean—exactly my type. I figure we'll get along. For the occasion, I've pulled out all the stops.

"What's your real name?" I say as we walk abreast toward Lincoln Center, bundled against the freezing cold. "It can't just be P."

"I will tell you later if I like you." She smiles. "You are a poet?"

"I am," I say, trying to stand up straight as I walk.

"That's cool. I have never seen a live poet. Since you are one, it would be interesting to tell me—what is it do you think is cordial love?"

I suspect she means "courtly." There is a slight language barrier.

"And," she adds carefully, "not what you think it is, but—what it is?"

"I'm not sure I understand," I say. "You mean, like, from the poetry of the troubadours? William of Aquitaine?"

She laughs loudly through her nose and points to me, cupping her hand to her mouth and bellowing so everyone on the sidewalk can hear. "Nerd alert!" I decide I like her.

“And you’re a physicist?” I say.

“I am.”

“That’s amazing.” I can’t think of a single thing to add.

A wailing toddler rolls by in a stroller, wrapped in a thick athleisure sarcophagus that writhes and kicks against the cold.

“How do you—uh—feel about kids?” I ask, boldly vaulting from flirty, awkward small talk into something else entirely. I promised myself I would be straightforward tonight. Not that I’m particularly interested in children—it just feels like a topic that a straightforward person would broach. “Do you want them?”

She raises her eyebrows but rolls with it. “I like children, but I would not like to own one.”

She pulls a cigarette out of her purse and lights it—odd, considering that in her profile she said she didn’t smoke tobacco. Do people lie about themselves on these things? She offers me one, and I accept, to give myself something to do with my hands for a few minutes.

“Do you go to the ballet often?” she says as we take our seats in David H. Koch Theater.

“No, actually—this is my first time. But Balanchine is supposed to be great.”

“I have seen his neoclassicals before,” she says. “Only once.”

The lights go down and a hush falls on the theater. On cue, like a firing squad, every elderly white person in the audience—the vast majority of the room—releases a wave of explosively wet, tubercular coughing.

In *Apollo*, the dancers click into a single organism, then just as smoothly dissemble and go about their louchely human privacy. Their faces dissolve into their limbs; the body here essentially becomes the face. A gigantic, sneering, zoetropic grave of joy. Calliope stomps off as if in two directions. Stravinsky seems to follow both of her.

In *Orpheus*, hell looks pretty fun. Some of the dancers come bearing exquisite bags on their heads and phalluses protruding from their shoulders, some come with an expensive and grueling education, but all of them know exactly where they're going.

At intermission on the balcony overlooking the fountain, a man holds crutches away from his torso at arm's length. "I don't need these!" he tells someone standing several yards away. Nearby, a trio of Italian tourists are deep in conversation, speaking and gesticulating heatedly, their breath floating up in the cold like tissues pulled from a box.

"Do you think they're talking about dissolving their bimonthly orgy or describing an extraordinarily beautiful lighthouse?" I say.

"Both!" She laughs. "I speak Italian."

"You speak Italian, but you're . . . Turkish?"

"I am!" she yells, slapping my arm, almost as surprised as I am that I'm right. "Good guess. But my Italian is pretty good."

"What were they really just talking about?"

"Fascism."

The bell chimes merrily, telling us to make our way back to our seats.

"I'm having a nice time," she says. When the lights go down again, she takes my hand and holds it in her lap.

In *Agon*, I don't pay attention to what happens. But whatever it is, I'm against it.

The next morning, sleepless but in an extremely good mood, I bring her coffee in bed. For the last few years, I've wondered if there is something wrong with me. Over the course of the last few hours, P. has emphatically suggested that the general area of wrongness I had been imagining might not be the problem.

"Thank you," she says, taking the hot mug with her fingertips. She kisses me lightly, and I wait for it to molt into something slower and more drawn out—her breath is bad, and I love it—but instead she turns, takes a sip, and squints. "But I think I might go out for coffee. I should be getting home anyway. Thank you for the evening. And morning." She begins getting dressed.

“This was really fun,” I say. “Do you want to hang out again, maybe?” She looks at me and squints, the way she did when she tasted the coffee.

“It was really fun.” She pauses. “You are a little cold?”

“Oh, are you cold? Sorry, the temperature in this building is really erratic—”

“No,” she says. “I mean I do not think you are ready for the things you think you want. Your heart is not open. It is best we don’t get attached. But I am glad we met.”

I am stunned. “I—how can you tell? That isn’t how I feel at all.”

“It’s not how you think you feel. It is how I know I feel.”

“I didn’t realize that. I’m sorry to hear it.”

We are quiet for a while.

“You never told me your name,” I say.

She ignores this. “I do not mean to be unkind.”

“No, it’s not that. I just—it’s not your fault.” My impulse is to leave it at that—but perhaps now is the time to say what I feel. I take a deep breath. “This is embarrassing, but I think I’ve put too much pressure on poetry and love to give my life meaning. It’s too much pressure for those two things. There needs to be a third thing.”

She nods. "I see. Have you considered money?"

"I don't think that's going to be the one."

"What about a riddle?" she says, putting on her coat. "A good riddle can be very exciting." She hesitates. "My name is Pinar."

I lock the door behind her and stand in my underwear.

Everything you do is a wound.

Scrolling through the news on my desktop at the office, I read that a Palestinian mother and her thirteen-year-old son have been killed by Israeli Defense Forces at an ongoing protest along the border in Gaza. Every Friday for nearly a year, Palestinian demonstrators have gathered at the fence to demand that they be allowed to return to their family homes in what is now Israel. The mother was shot and died at the scene; the boy was hit in the head with a tear gas canister and succumbed to his injuries days later.

My face feels numb, then hot. What, I wonder, would I do if someone did this to my mother?

Then, from a different part of my screen, I receive an email notification requesting a description for an event promoting the latest book by a world-famous "thought leader" and corporate guru—a "data-driven" book about the scientifically proven benefits of talking to strangers.

And how, I wonder, my knuckles going white on the handle of my coffee mug, does this data make you feel?

I call Will. He doesn't pick up. I call Ruth. She doesn't pick up. I call Lucy. She doesn't pick up.

I decide to call my mom.

"What's wrong?" she says when she picks up.

"Nothing," I lie. "Just calling to say hi."

"Oh. Well—hi!"

"How was your day?"

"Let's see. I was having lunch with an old friend today, someone I used to work with—you know, actually, it was pretty weird. We're catching up about this and that, and suddenly he just casually drops—he recently discovered he's a *sex* addict! He started going to meetings and everything. I couldn't believe it. I mean, it's great, he's working on himself. Anyway, the kicker is that after deciding he wanted to make a change in his life—I'll spare you the gruesome details, but let's just say he was going through a lot of lotion—he figured all of this out because he started reading books about something called Radical Honesty. Radical Honesty! And then he takes one of these books out—Lord knows where it's been—and slides it across the table and tells me he'd like me to have it. Can you believe that? I said, 'Uh, no thanks, hon—I don't want to be that honest!' Anyway, he's a nice—"

"Listen, sorry—actually, something is wrong."

"I knew it," she says, her voice sharpening to a blade.

"I read a horrible story in the news, and it made me wonder—this is an awful question."

"You can ask me anything."

"If I were at a protest, and I was shot and killed by a cop, or a soldier—what would you do?"

On the other end of the line, I hear my dad washing dishes.

"Are you in trouble?" she says, quietly.

"No, it's nothing like that. Please don't worry."

"That is the single worst thing that could happen to a parent."

"I know. I'm sorry to make you think about it. But I'd like to know. What would you do?"

In the background, my dad is faintly whistling "Bridge over Troubled Water."

"Honestly?" She sighs. "I'd do what any mother would do. I would try to imagine that cop or soldier's mother." She pauses. "Or I would hunt him down to the ends of the earth and kill him with my bare hands."

"Our friends being friends only in the light of an agreeable folly which travels with us through life and to which we readily accommodate ourselves, but which at the bottom of our hearts we know to be no more reasonable than the delusion of the man who talks to the furniture because he believes that it is alive." (Proust, *Time Regained*)

I finish *In Search of Lost Time.* It took almost exactly a year. An interval that, I recall thinking a year ago, might change me.

FEBRUARY

A shadow with lipstick on its teeth.

A face that has no end.

Surveying the copy I've submitted, my Senior Content Adjuster says, "Oh, I don't know, D__. Could you try again? This is a bit *froid*, don't you think?"

Outside the conference room window, snow gathers on the buildings.

There's a difference between writing a poem and writing poetry—a poem always ends, but poetry keeps going. And if I try too hard to write one, I inadvertently end up writing the other. Perhaps there's a similar split between performing labor and doing work.

I file into Bret Stephens King Concert Hall with the entire staff at my workplace for diversity training. We all settle into our seats.

"Thank you for being here," says the white woman facilitating into a headset microphone. "What an amazing institution this is. I'm excited for us to do this work together. I'd like to start with a general question. What kinds of communities do you feel are welcome in this workplace? There are no wrong answers. Don't be shy."

A brief silence. "Well, this is a Jewish institution, of course, so Jews are welcome here," someone says. "All Jews."

"That's great," says the white woman.

"Anyone who is connected to the survivors of genocide," says the rabbi.

"Very good," says the white woman. "Anyone else?"

"We serve all communities here," someone says. "From people interested in jewelry-making classes to people interested in water polo to people interested in current events. From the toddler community to the elderly. Sorry, I mean individuals who are over sixty-five."

"Ethiopians!" someone yells out.

"Wow. Thank you. Now I'd like to pose a different question. Are there any communities that you would say are not welcome here?"

No one speaks. As the seconds pass, they seem to expand and contract, as if they are breathing. I turn around, pretending to stretch, looking behind me in the concert hall. The executives, sitting together in the back, are stone-faced. But there are subtle variations—all of them are stone-faced in slightly different ways. One is dreamily still, perhaps vaguely pleased. One whose mouth is slightly downturned seems primed, serenely and confidently, just behind his unblinking eyes, for physical violence. Another, upon closer inspection, has delicately knit her brow—she is worried, her face turned toward the stage but her eyes cast down, as if in prayer, to her phone.

I glance around at the rest of the room and realize I am not alone—many of us have discreetly contorted ourselves toward this back row.

"Great!" says the white woman. "This concludes diversity training. See you next year!"

SPRING NOTEBOOK, 2019

MARCH

February is always ending early, but March is pure delay.

Parable of the Final Line

There he was, supine, taking his ease in the premature March clover, reading a horse poem.

And what a slippery horse poem it was proving itself to be—as he increasingly suspected, the closer he got to the final line, that it might actually be more about dogs.

"How are you feeling?" I ask Ruth on FaceTime. I am at Will's house, with him and Lucy. We are finishing dinner. Ruth is sitting in a bathtub filled with ice.

"Bad," she says. "Very bad. I can barely walk anywhere. I can't think straight. My entire body itches. The only thing that makes it better is sitting in an ice bath. It's called cholestasis. Apparently my liver is leaking poison into my veins, so I itch all over but there's no rash. It's a nightmare."

"Jesus," Will says.

"I'm sorry, Ruth," Lucy says. "That sounds awful."

"They're inducing labor in early April. It's a fucking miracle that human beings have survived this long, if this is what it takes to bring one into the world. This is hell."

"They're inducing labor? What if we came out to LA for it?" Lucy says.

"I could do that," I say. "I have the vacation days."

"You guys don't have to do that," Ruth says.

"But we want to," Will says. "To meet the baby. And be there for you."

Ruth's lips are turning blue.

"You also have to meet Homer," she says.

In the Turkish language, I read while idly browsing Wikipedia in my cubicle, there is an entire grammatical tense for gossip. Every sentence begins: "Allegedly . . ."

A public debate that plays out in the exchange of cruelty.

A panel discussion that plays out in silence.

A poem that plays out in the spinal cord, muscles, glands, and ducts.

A private conversation that plays out in public.

"I read in *The New York Times* that a poet named W. S. Merwin died last week," my mom says on the phone. "Did you know him?"

"Merwin was ninety. He lived on a rare palm reservation that he started in Hawaii. I obviously didn't know him."

"You should have sent him an email," my dad says. "You had a lot in common. You're both poets. You both like trees. And he was very accomplished. Too bad. Sad, actually."

"I've never really connected with Merwin's poetry, honestly. I find most of it pretty boring."

"Boring?" my mom says. "This Merwin guy wrote fifty books, apparently! He saves a bunch of rare trees, wins two Pulitzer Prizes, and you're calling him boring?"

"He worked hard for that," my dad says. "He put elbow grease into it."

"Look, I can't help it—Merwin is boring! Some of the poems are fine but a lot of it is about saving the whales and Buddhism for white people! I do love *The Lice*. Does that make you feel better?"

"You think W. S. Merwin is boring, suddenly you hate whales and Buddhism, but you love lice?"

"It's the name of one of his books. The only one I like. *The Lice*."

"What a weird title," my mom says. "Why do you always have to like weird stuff?"

"Guys," I say, "Merwin lived for almost a century and died on a tract of earthly paradise among trees that he loved. It doesn't matter that I think his poems are boring. He had a beautiful life. He doesn't need you to defend him. What is the point of this lecture?"

"The point is," my dad says carefully, "he couldn't have died in that nice forest without the elbow grease."

APRIL

I am shopping for a baby gift for Ruth, alone, at a complete loss. What does one get for a baby? Perhaps a small hat? They all have animal ears: bear ears, fox ears, rabbit ears. I choose fox ears.

What is it about us, I wonder, waiting in the checkout line, that we want our babies to be decoratively ornamented with the auditory hardware of the forest?

Everyone knows what a baby comes out of. What we haven't considered is: what does a baby go *in*?

I try to guess who is texting me by the rate and frequency of the buzzes in my pocket. Often I am right. Ruth: one buzz. Lucy: also just one, but somehow melodic. Will: five in quick succession. My mom: two. My dad: either one or seven—often, somehow, both one and seven.

Tonight it's one buzz. A selfie, in a maternity ward, followed by

> hi from hell ❤

What do the stars look like tonight? I think Ruth would want to know. I walk outside to see, but it's overcast—none are visible.

A few hours later I get another text.

> she's here

The next morning, we fly to LA.

Parable of Exodus Rental Car

"I make things happen," says the woman behind the counter at Exodus Rental Car outside LAX. "Don't worry." Our car is not on the lot. I am trying to be chill.

"Did we have to go to the absolute cheapest rental car place you could find online?" Lucy says quietly. Will is fuming.

"Don't be that way. This is part of the adventure."

"Since when did adventure become the base unit of all human experience?" Will says.

The woman behind the counter takes my license and enters my information into the system. Then she frowns and looks up at me. "Are you Jewish?"

I don't like where this is going. I take a deep breath and smile. "Yes, actually."

She beams. "Me too. That must be why I'm hooking you up."

She tosses me the keys to a Nissan Versa.

LA is heaven, or maybe just everything I need from heaven. Unlike New York it feels, very occasionally, abandoned. A perfect husk of a perfect husk. Spray-painted on an overpass as we drive into Los Feliz:

MAKE AMERICA NOTHING AGAIN

Parable of Surfer Girl

When we get to the hospital, Lucy and Will go straight up to Ruth's room. I stop in the cafeteria for a cup of coffee.

I see Chester sitting alone, catatonically happy, staring into space, blissed out on new-dad endorphins. I haven't seen him in person since grad school. He gets up and gives me a bear hug.

"What's it like?" I say.

He rubs his eyes and considers. "One minute it's all *here*," he says, holding a fist out. "My entire focus is on Ruth. And then the baby comes out"—he opens his palm—"and suddenly a *there* is here too. And you realize—that *there* could go anywhere." He throws his hand into the air. "I think I need more coffee."

Up in the room, Lucy hands her to me. Less than a day old, she rests her head on my shoulder, and her cheek pools around the totality of her dreaming face. I don't know how much time passes like that, and never will. If you touch her, she ripples.

I hand her to Will. The little squeak she makes in response to motion is all she says. Ruth sits on a bag of ice as Lucy rubs her back. "Guys," Ruth says, "I done been shook." Will hands her to Chester. Chester holds this tiny self in his arms and then hands her back to Ruth. The five of us sing "Surfer Girl" to her as she sleeps.

Is it here from where I'll see you there?

On the morning I turn thirty-four, I head out to the Santa Monica Mountains alone before dawn. I hit the trail as the light is a dusky blue and get to the top of a ridge just as it is turning from washed-out turquoise to red. On my left, at the horizon over the Pacific Ocean, as the sun hits from behind me, I can just barely make out the dull, watery edge of the planet's curve. Turning right, shadows scratched like musical notation across the mountains, I realize that I am facing the precise direction I was driving from last summer.

What are these three hundred miles of leaping pink light I never traveled through?

"Come here, Homer!" Ruth says when we arrive for dinner. "Say hi to your new friends!"

The most gnarled, ancient cat I have ever seen hobbles into the room. He is gaunt and looks slightly melted. In the place where his eyes should be, two smooth craters of fur flank his little nose. He looks extracted directly from a nightmare, then devoured again to be redigested back into dream, much the way a cat will eat its own vomit.

"What's wrong with his eyes?" Lucy says, looking pale.

"He doesn't have them. He was born with a degenerative disease. A vet sewed his sockets shut when he was a kitten to prevent infection. That's why I knew his name was Homer. The blind poet. Isn't he precious?"

None of us speak.

After dinner, we sit around the table talking. Now that Ashbery is dead, we wonder, who are the best living poets? We all get to make two nominations.

"Obviously Alice Notley. And Kim Hyesoon," Will says.

"Claudia Rankine and—no, Claudia Rankine is too obvious. I'm going to say Robyn Schiff and Julian Talamantez Brolaski," Lucy says.

"You just picked three!" I say.

"Straight to jail for me."

"Can I participate even though I don't write poetry anymore?" Chester says, holding the baby.

"Of course, dude," Will says. "We're not gatekeepers. Let's hear it."

"Raúl Zurita and Louise Glück."

"What a weird pairing," Will says. "Those are completely incoherent choices."

"Good taste can be incoherent," Ruth says, kissing Chester.

"Glück gives me the creeps," I say.

"I like her spareness," Chester says, confidently. "Always have."

"What do you like about Zurita?"

"Skywriting 'MY GOD IS A WOUND' over New York?" Chester says. "I don't know, man. It's hardcore."

"Glück writes about divorce and sad flowers," Will says. "Zurita writes about being imprisoned and tortured by fascists."

"Pinochet's regime ended, but Glück is imprisoned and tortured by fascists to this day," Ruth says. "Male poets."

"Who are your two?" Chester says, unfazed, turning to me.

"Lisa Robertson and Nathaniel Mackey," I say. I turn to Ruth.

"Jorie Graham and Ben Lerner," Ruth says.

"Ben Lerner shouldn't count," I say. "He sold out. He's basically a novelist now."

"What is your problem?" Lucy says. "The novel is just a form, same as a sonnet or free verse. Do you like Ben Lerner's novels?"

"Yes," I say into my lap. "I love them."

"Cuck," Will mutters.

"There are lots of great living poets who are indisputably poets," I say. "Lyn Hejinian. Bernadette Mayer."

"If you write poems, you're a poet," Lucy says. "But Solmaz Sharif might be the only one right around our age who isn't insufferable." Everyone nods.

"Except for the people in this room," Ruth says. "You all are my favorite living poets."

"We are insufferable," Lucy says, "but I agree."

"Our poems are completely different," I say. "What unifies our school of poetry?"

We mull on this for a moment.

"As poets?" Will says. "We are all very stable geniuses."

Even though I walk through the valley of the shadow of nope, I will fear no yeah.

In the airport as we are about to board our red-eye home to New York, I make the mistake of checking my work email. Scrolling through the sales reports and departmental announcements about the status of the clogged toilet by the executive conference room, I open a message from a programmer requesting an event description for a lecture by a prominent former US statesman of European Jewish extraction.

His biography is well-known. After emigrating to the United States to escape the Nazi regime, he went on to an illustrious career in academia and the US government, rising to the pinnacles of power in Washington, landing on the covers of many prominent magazines, winning a Nobel Peace Prize, committing an impressive litany of war crimes leading to millions of civilian deaths, providing a mordantly jovial recurring presence on decades of late-night TV, his cherubic face slowly sinking further into the depths of his neck through the late autumn of his years. He is widely despised all over the world for the bloodshed and destruction resulting from his policies, but at my workplace this bespectacled mass murderer is being booked for an annual endowed lecture series for prominent figures from across the global Jewish diaspora called the Children of Light. The programmer is asking for an event description by the beginning of May.

“Dude, we’re about to board,” Will says. “What is happening on your phone?”

I am in the middle seat on the flight. Will is asleep to my right on the aisle, mouth agape, eyes covered with a mask. Lucy sits to my left, gasping with laughter over a film about two British men who exchange impressions of celebrities over thousand-dollar lunches. I tap her arm. She removes her earbuds.

"What are we doing?" I say.

"What are we doing? I'm watching the best Michael Caine impression I've ever seen. What are you doing?"

"No, I mean—what does poetry do?"

A deep sigh. "I don't know, man," she says, lifting the window shade. The sky is full of towering blue clouds. "I'm not sure I buy that line of questioning."

"It doesn't bother you that the country is about two seconds away from becoming a full-blown fascist death cult and we've organized our lives around writing poems for one another that almost no one else will ever read?"

She shakes her head. "Poetry is the thing we know how to do for one another. Spending your time writing it doesn't make you bad—or good, for that matter."

In the window behind her, disparate patches of a large cloud flicker with submerged lightning.

Dream, 4/26

I am holding a meeting in a boardroom. All my words are assembled around a large conference table. I am making a speech. At the end, I say, "I couldn't have done this without you."

One of the words pulls his arms inside his sweatshirt and hugs his knees like a child.

MAY

Nothing

A poem called "Nothing"
In which it is described

Can I ask who's calling?

Back at the office, the programmer emails me again.

May 10, 2019, 3:01 PM

Hi D__, just circling back on that Children of Light event description. The talent needs to approve the copy before we go live. We don't want to keep him waiting.

Thx

I walk to the water cooler. The rabbi is there, filling his Nalgene. A thought occurs to me.

"Rabbi—sorry to bother you, but do you have a moment?"

"How could you bother me?" he says, his knuckles white as he twists the cap on the water bottle.

"Forgive me for asking this out of the blue."

"Please. This is my job. Ask me anything."

"Do you believe in God?"

He is silent for a moment.

"That isn't a stupid question. It's a profound one. The answer is no."

I am surprised. "You don't?"

"Belief is interesting. Is God real? Through this question, one arrives at belief—belief therefore always begins in doubt. I don't *believe* in God. I am *certain* of God. I have experienced his power. I know who his children are—and who they aren't." He wags his eyebrows and grins conspiratorially. A copy machine whirrs at the end of the hall.

"Thank you," I say. "That's helpful."

He nods.

I walk back to my desk and send a reply to the programmer's email. It is unoriginal.

> May 10, 2019, 3:16 PM
>
> I would prefer not to.
>
> D__

I receive no reply before heading home for the weekend.

On my way home, I get off a stop early to walk through Prospect Park. As I enter the big meadow, it begins to rain. A chill sets in. The astonished worms slither from the earth.

Worms woweth under dew, soil, and cloud. All my life I wondered at what. But at what they woweth, I know now.

Evil and beauty need each other.

The following Sunday, I receive an email from HR on my personal account telling me not to come into the office on Monday—I have been placed on probationary leave for three weeks while a recent incident involving my performance and conduct is investigated. Under probationary status, my salary will be withheld, but my insurance coverage will remain in place, for now.

I look up a dentist in my network and book an appointment for the following week.

As the hygienist cleans my teeth, she scolds me—it's clear that I haven't been flossing every day. Also, since my last visit—years ago—apparently my last wisdom tooth has emerged. It is not infected, as my dad feared it would be, but it must be extracted. The dentist can fit me in that afternoon. I should arrange for someone to pick me up, bring me home, and look after me until the anesthesia wears off.

Imagine a novel consisting of several variations on the Orpheus and Eurydice myth—one for every tooth in the mouth.

Each tooth on the top row represents a different poem about snakes Eurydice wrote on Earth before one did her in. Each tooth on the bottom row represents a different lullaby about sleepy three-headed dogs Orpheus had to sing before Cerberus finally closed all six of his eyes.

Each tooth on the top row represents a different sex act Eurydice had been looking forward to trying once again on Earth before Orpheus's big, stupid face turned around. Each tooth on the bottom row represents a different sex act Eurydice had loved in Hades before Orpheus came down there and almost ruined everything.

Each tooth on the top row represents a different song in Orpheus's repertoire, if you don't count the ones the plants told him to sing. Each tooth on the bottom row represents a moment when Orpheus checked his phone the day after Eurydice was gone.

Will and Lucy are standing over me in a bright waiting room full of chairs. They look concerned. "I don't think they did it," I say, blood dribbling from my mouth. "Something's still there."

No poem lives in the throat—it only passes through. A windpipe thus receives its paycheck—meaning—and the teeth a taste of the underworld. "Since to each meaning savour we apply."

Parable of Midnight

When I tell them about my employment limbo, my parents deploy a strategic silence—they know when not to push me. All my dad asks is if I'd like to meet him for coffee in my neighborhood.

Brooklyn is in full bloom the day he drives in, flowering trees dropping syllabic petals, a shower of them fluttering around us like a poem you read once in deep pleasure before forgetting every line forever. It feels as if winter will never come again.

"I've been excited for this!" he says as he sits down. "And normally I'm a pretty calm guy."

"Cut to the chase," I say.

"Was it really worth it?"

"We don't know if I'm going to lose my job," I sigh. "But yes, honestly, if I'm fired for refusing to launder the reputation of a war criminal, I can live with that."

“And what’s your plan if that happens?”

“I’ll find another job.”

“And at this other job,” he says, stirring his coffee, “do you think they *won’t* ask you to launder the reputation of a war criminal?”

I stare at him.

“This was your decision, and I respect it,” he goes on. “But it seems to me—you’re acting like nothing can happen to you.”

This I consider.

“Did you know my parents were from this part of Brooklyn?” he says, out of nowhere.

He abruptly launches into two family legends.

The first I’ve heard before. In 1911, at sixteen, speaking no English and with no money, my great-grandmother left her parents, ten siblings, and their dirt-floor family home in a village in Ukraine and came to New York in search of an education. Shortly thereafter, her family was slaughtered in anti-Jewish Russian pogroms. She never returned. As my grandfather was growing up in Brooklyn, she told him to find a trade that exercised his mind—because when the men come for you, if they leave you alive, they cut off your hands.

The second story is new to me. One New Year’s Eve, during the war, my grandmother’s parents were throwing a party for their friends in their Brooklyn home not far from where we are drinking coffee. There was food and music, and it was very cold. My father’s mother—trapped, bored—stuck her head out her bedroom window to feel a bit of icy air. Two young men walked by on the street below. On a whim, she yelled out, "Do you boys want to come in and dance?" One of them no one in my family remembers; the other was my grandfather.

Later, when I am alone in my apartment, I reflect on these stories. I understand—I think—the significance of the first. But why did he tell the second?

The way my grandfather dragged his finger over a page when he read to me, letter by letter.

Fate is a line. It doesn't break into words—it breaks into pieces.

A watched phone never buzzes; a surveilled siience never buzzes; a swatted bee buzzes until it doesn't; a partygoer absent from the open window never buzzes you in; you didn't hear a fly buzz when you died, because you're alive; a buzz is never the text you want to receive when you want to receive it. But a ring comes just in time.

I receive permission from security to stop by my desk to gather a few personal items while I await word from HR. I have never been here on a weekend before. The office is deserted.

Looking out over the vacant hive of cubicles, sun streaking through the windows, I shake my head. My productivity could double if it were always like this—quiet, empty, full of light.

Hell 2

It was in the right place
It must have been the wrong time
It faced the music
It had a thousand faces
Its body was saying let's go
Its heart was saying no
It let the bodies hit the floor
It would do anything for love
It wouldn't do that
It turned a winnowing fan into an oar
It went south fast
Its surface was just visible core
It was a show about nothing
It was written
It was lit
It believed I could fly
It couldn't believe it wasn't
It was one man's ceiling and another man's floor
It had a nice ring to it
It was the best of times
It was the best of times
It was best-laid plans
It takes a real man
Its suns out, guns out
It was snowing
It was going to snow
It felt so New York
It guided my hand
It drew a line in the sand

NOTES AND ACKNOWLEDGMENTS

The passages quoted from Proust were translated by Lydia Davis (*Swann's Way*), C. K. Scott Moncrieff and Terence Kilmartin (*Within a Budding Grove*, *Sodom and Gomorrah*, *The Captive*, *The Fugitive*, and *Time Regained*), and Mark Treharne (*The Guermantes Way*).

The Copywriter began in 2017 as a long poem exploring the formal and lyric possibilities of writing in notebooks. Rachel Mannheimer read an early draft and was the first to suggest that it might be a novel; Kathy Belden at Scribner subsequently took a chance on it; both of them, along with Madison Thân, offered invaluable sentence-level guidance on every subsequent draft. I am beyond grateful to all three for their brilliance, patience, and vision.

Thank you to everyone at Scribner; to Elif Batuman; to my agent, Jim Rutman, and everyone at Sterling Lord Literistic; and to everyone at the residency programs at Norton Island and the T. S. Eliot House.

Thank you to the editors of *Annulet*, *The Brooklyn Rail*, *The Canary*, *Changes Review*, *Chicago Review*, *The Columbia Review*, *Copenhagen*, *Denver Quarterly*, *McSweeney's*, *The New Republic*, *Ocean State Review*, *The Paris Review* Daily, *Practice Catalogue*, *Pigeon Pages*, *Prelude*, *R&R*, *The Spectacle*, *Volume*, and *The Yale Review*, where portions of this book first appeared, often in significantly different forms.

Thank you to the friends who read this in multiple iterations over the years and whose conversation, generosity, wisdom, and intellect are reflected throughout, particularly Callie Garnett, Chris Schlegel, David Gorin, Henry Chapman, Jake Fournier, Jean Garnett, Jessica Laser, Maggie Millner, and Margaret Ross; to Adrienne Raphel, Ashley Colley, Bridget Talone, Colby Sommerville, Katie Fowley, Rawaan Alkhatib, and Sara Deniz Akant; to Andrés Millan, Ariel Lewiton, Bernard Schwartz, Brittany Dennison, Catherine Pollock, Elena Saavedra Buckley, Elisabeth Benjamin, Emile Mosseri, Emily Sieu Liebowitz, Emily Skillings, Eri Linsker, Eric Dean Wilson, G.C. Waldrep, Hannah Zeavin, Jeff Nagy, Katie Taylor, Kristen Radtke, Kyle McCarthy, Laraine Perri, Laura MacMillan, Lisa Wells, Mark Mayer, Micah Bateman, Megan Fernandes, Megan Nolan, Noah Warren, Rebecca Zweig, Ricky Maldonado, Rob Schlegel, Sara Nicholson, Sarah Friedland, Simone Kearney, Sophie Dahlin, Ted Mathys, Zach Pace, and Zaina Arafat; to Hannah Kingsley-Ma; and to my family.

ABOUT THE AUTHOR

Daniel Poppick is the author of the poetry collections *Fear of Description*, a winner of the National Poetry Series, and *The Police*. His writing appears in *The New Yorker*, *The Paris Review*, *The New Republic*, *The Yale Review*, *BOMB*, and elsewhere. He lives in Brooklyn.